KW-360-961

For Irene.
We traveled and loved the life we had.

Algeria is an incredible country
with beautiful places to explore,
and people who are welcoming
and hospitable.

This is a work of fiction. Names, characters and incidents are the
products of the author's imagination. Any resemblance to actual
persons, living or dead, or actual events is purely coincidental.

PART ONE

PROLOGUE

Death comes in many forms and creeps up on you without warning, then leaves you shattered and reeling. It also leaves an aftermath—weeks, months, even years following those left behind. The heartache never disappears. It only hides in secret places of your mind, surfacing as memories return and then recede.

The memories of the life you lived force you to re-examine and question why. A more mature you would have . . . but all these "what-ifs" are pointless, as they only bury you in further grief and despair. But no matter how hard you try, they still bubble up to the surface and capture you unawares.

Walking on the beach on a cold, windswept day, a wave of emotion smashed into me. Hands shaking and vision blurred, it forced me to my knees. Barely noticing the wind whipping up the sand and the decay of a half-eaten seagull, one dull and lifeless eye glaring up at the world it no longer lives in.

I wept for what had been. Memories of our time together haunting me. We had loved and enjoyed life, but had been drawn into a darker, more dangerous place. Why is this greyness torturing me now with recollections of so long ago? Algeria had been bright and warm and invigorating. You had been so full of life, and yet . . .

Rosie's passionate licking of my hand, her wagging tail, and her bright, brown eyes looking intently at me gave me some sense of another life. I could see a look of . . . what? Concern? Love? Yes. But something more, an inner awareness. She knew this was not me, and she needed to bring me back to her and to life itself. She licked and licked. Her hot, wet tongue re-awakened a sense of living and of the world around me: It was bitterly cold. I sat up, then struggled to stand. Two deep brown eyes willing me—intent on reviving me. "Come on, let's go," I said. I staggered home, exhausted, and collapsed on the sofa.

Algeria. Those memories of forty years ago flooded back. *Sue sitting at a café table, laughing and talking with young Frenchmen. Riding horses on the beach, galloping on the sand: innocent and free.* I shuddered and reached for the bottle. Alcohol numbed my brain and stifled the intensity of feeling. *Moussa smiling and reaching out his hand to greet me.* I drank, gulping down the rum. It burned the back of my throat, sat heavily on my stomach, and made me feel less human.

◆ ◆ ◆

The phone's incessant, urgent ringing woke me—hungover, my mind hazy and numb. "UNKNOWN CALLER." A Vancouver number. *Shit. Who the fuck?* I swiped.

"Dave? David? It's Farid."

Those memories. The enormity shocked me awake.

"Farid?" Inwardly, I groaned, feeling intense dread mixed with heartbreaking excitement. I croaked, "Where are you?"

"In Vancouver. Can we meet?"

Farid had tracked me down. We lost contact when he had been offered a job in New York. Algeria had been fun, stimulating, dangerous, and the awakening of a more intense sexuality. I'd suppressed those feelings in recesses of my brain I hadn't wanted to reopen. They were too painful, but part of me wanted to pick at the scars, to see what's buried beneath.

I met him in the hotel lobby. He was older, of course—we both were—but he was still good-looking. We hugged and it felt good.

"Where is Sue?"

I shook my head. "I can't . . . Later."

I looked at the crowded reception: tourists off the cruise ships milled around, talking incessantly.

Farid interrupted our awkward silence. "Come to my room. We can talk. Have dinner sent up—a bottle of wine."

"Yes," I said in a faint voice, fearing the inevitability of it all: The opening of those wounds and the blood-letting of memories.

The view was impressive—overlooking the harbour and across the bay to North Vancouver and its snow-capped mountains—but I wasn't sure what to say or how to start.

Farid interrupted my thoughts. "Those years in Algeria. Have you forgotten? Liz, Moussa . . ." He stopped and looked at me.

Moussa. His name crashed into my consciousness to re-awaken deep, intense feelings. "No. I haven't forgotten."

"We were—such good friends." His voice faltered. Farid sounded desperate—lost. I wanted to revisit the past but was terrified of taking the first step. *I could have said no, but we were drawn into playing their games, and really, what did it all mean to us?*

We spent a few precious days together, talking late into the night and going for long walks in Stanley Park. Reminiscing about our shared past and walking the seawall freed us both. We revisited the joy and grief through joking, laughing, and getting emotional again.

Farid helped me readjust. I couldn't tell him about Sue. It was still too raw. But Moussa? As we talked, I felt the lifting of a heavy weight—a burden not of guilt but regret.

◆ ◆ ◆

As far as the Algerian government is concerned, this incident never happened: A blip on the radar too small to even have registered and easy to deny. Farid is not his real name. He never came to Vancouver. The rest of us? Nobody cares.

ONE

Summer, 1978

"Good morning. This is Mr. David Graham; I'm phoning to confirm the time of my interview."

"Mr. Graham, your interview was yesterday. The headmaster will not see you now," the school secretary informed me in one of those commanding, upper-middle-class English accents. The line went dead.

Later, I realized I had been dismissed from England. Admittedly, I had confused the dates, planning to spend the weekend visiting friends in London and felt it was better to have the interview on Friday instead of Thursday. But maybe fate had intervened on my behalf. The job was to teach English Lit. and Drama in a private high school in southern England. Thinking about it, I know it wouldn't have been right. At twenty-four, freedom and adventure awaited, rather than stultifying boredom. I had never been abroad and wanted something better in life.

Back to the *Times Ed*, the rag for jobs. In the overseas section, I saw one: *The Algerian Ministry of Education requires native speakers to teach English in local high schools.*

I remember the day and date well: Friday, September 8, 1978. Checking in at the Air Algérie desk, I realized this was a new beginning—my first real job.

At Heathrow Airport, I met two other passengers, Josephine and Cameron, who were also flying to Algiers to become teachers. Josephine being a fellow Geordie, we chatted away, becoming firm friends in a short time.

After the relative calm of Heathrow, Algiers Airport was noisy and chaotic. However, we were met and joined by a group of other young teachers. We clambered onto retired American school buses, which took us up past crumbling white houses with lush rose, pink, purple, and orange bougainvillea cascading over the white plastered walls. Trees of yellow-flowered mimosa, growing wild and luxuriantly, created splashes of colour in the evening light. The bus windows were open, allowing the intense aromas of North Africa to assail our senses. The scents of flowers and wood fires, the sea air, and roasting meat permeated the air. A desire to explore blossomed in my heart. I felt alive and wanted to fully inhabit this exotic and appealing world of North Africa.

The Ministry of Education had prepared three days of orientation to educate us about the country and prepare us for the days, weeks, and months ahead. During those first few days, I chatted with quite a few others employed to be English Foreign Language teachers in the high schools. They were primarily young and excited, and many of them would have made excellent companions. However, I had drawn the joker, Seamus, the other teacher assigned to Bou Saâda. He was short with unkempt red hair and a long, scraggly red beard. He came across as supremely self-confident and laughed at his own jokes. My new friend, Josephine, was immediately dismissive of him.

"Transfer," she said. "Come to Hadjout with Cameron and me. It'll be fun."

But I didn't want to transfer. I had been assigned to a school in a small town on the edge of the Sahara and imagined myself a British explorer entering an exotic, romantic, and challenging land. I'd spent hours in the library reading about the Sahara, searching for every reference to Bou Saâda. I felt passionate about my assigned town and becoming a teacher there.

◆ ◆ ◆

After three days, they gave us travel permits to our towns. I took a taxi to the central bus station but had no idea what Seamus had planned. In fact, I hadn't spoken to him since meeting him during the orientation.

The ticket office was crowded, hot, and full of people shouting, pushing, and desperate to buy a ticket. I stood quietly in a long queue behind the Bou Saâda window. An hour later, in my schoolboy French, I declared my destination to the ticket-seller and gave over my travel permit. We each spoke a different version of French—mine a schoolboy French while the older man behind the window spoke a patios Algerian French—making it challenging to understand each other.

"This permit. Not ticket. Not possible."

"Look, Ministry of Education ticket Bou Saâda."

"Not possible."

"Not possible?" I repeated in disbelief. The heat and stuffiness added to my frustration, as the ceiling fan was merely circulating hot air. But even worse, the man behind was trying to shove me out of the queue in his urgency to get a ticket.

"Please, I am teacher."

"Not possible."

This was getting farcical. "Why?" I cried out in desperation.

"This express bus. Ministry paper, not express bus." He didn't look sympathetic. It was hot and he was dealing with an unruly crowd of frustrated passengers. Why would he have time for an imbecile like me who didn't understand the basics of ticket-buying in Algeria? He looked at me impatiently.

"Oh," I pushed back at the Arab behind me, who smelled of unwashed sheep. "How much?"

"Window number four." He pointed in the general direction, his last words to me, "Change for ticket."

At that moment, I was triumphantly dislodged by the man behind. Defeated, I went to window four where there were fewer people. I paid a supplement costing fifty percent of the ticket. So much for travel passes, as all the buses to Bou Saâda were express. Armed with a ticket, I felt confident again. I deposited my luggage and had almost three hours before the bus left at two-thirty p.m. Then, reading a notice I hadn't seen before, I realized the left-luggage office didn't open again until two. I shrugged. I was hungry and reckoned there was enough time to get something to eat. The bus station was near the port. Looking up, you could see the white colonial buildings extending in a wide semi-circle around the bay and into the hills.

I found the nearest, cleanest-looking restaurant and ate fresh fish in a thick tomato sauce with rice on the side—delicious.

Back at the bus station, a crowd had formed in front of the left-luggage office. I learned about power then. The British secretary had dismissed me so cursorily, and now we were under the control of the man in charge of the left-luggage office. We were an unruly, sweaty mob demanding to get in and reclaim our bags. He shouted and presumably said something in Arabic like, "I won't give you your bags until you all back off and form an orderly line."

We backed off, and the attendant checked our tickets then passed the bags over. One man shouted. The attendant screamed at him and sent him to the back of the queue. We were all silent: All of us in his power.

Half-past two must have been departure time for many of the buses. Crowds ran toward each bus as it arrived, and people tried to jump on before the bus had even stopped It looked like far more people had tickets than there were seats.

Then I heard people yelling "Bou Saâda" as a bus arrived. A mass of people hurled themselves at the arriving dark orange

Mercedes coach and followed it, struggling to climb through the open door. I waited, standing rather forlorn with my ticket in my hand, and tried to work out how to get on a bus that looked massively oversold. The conductor noticed me in the crowd of shouting individuals. Feeling sorry for me, he motioned me forward, checked my ticket, and gave my suitcases to a boy who disappeared around the back. He then allowed me to enter the relative calm and tranquility of the bus.

I sat at the back next to a window, intending to look at the countryside as we drove south. A young Algerian woman got on and sat down next to me. She said something I either didn't hear or didn't understand. I looked at her, but this made me feel uncomfortable. From what I had read, Algerian women didn't talk to strangers. Ignoring her, I looked out the window.

Once away from the city, people settled down to doze fitfully, but the air-con was on full blast, and after a while, it got chilly. This strange woman threw her woollen cloak over the two of us. I smiled and said, "*Merci*," to show I appreciated her gesture.

However, after a few minutes, her hand sought mine under the cover of the cloth. She squeezed it. I self-consciously looked around: could anyone see this? Her hand explored my body. Intrigued, I reciprocated, as it seemed almost rude not to. Here we were, hurtling through the late afternoon. While my fellow passengers tried to sleep, a young Algerian woman was feeling me up. But I felt uncomfortable and eventually pushed her hand away and closed my eyes, pretending to sleep.

Later on, the bus stopped, and I woke to find the conductor shouting at my fellow passenger, telling her to get off the bus. I looked out the window and could see a *bled*, a poor village in the middle of nowhere. She pleaded tearfully with him, and I gleaned from her mixed French and Arabic that she could only pay for part of her journey and had a sick mother she was going to see. I quietly slipped her all the dinars I had in change. In a voice of triumph, she proclaimed loudly to the conductor something along the lines of, "You see how this foreigner behaves? He does not even know me, and yet he gives me money for my ticket so I can continue my journey and see my sick mother, who is on the point of death."

Everyone turned to look at me, and a couple of the young men leered. Embarrassed, I looked out the window, but I was pleased that the crisis was over. As the bus resumed its journey, we passed a few shacks and a muddy, potholed main street. No wonder the thought of being stranded there had filled her with dread.

She got off at another sad village. I hoped she would be all right, but she hadn't spoken to me the entire time.

TWO

After a few more stops at poor communities, the bus pulled off the road in the middle of nowhere and the driver turned off the engine. He said something in Arabic to the passengers and disappeared. The bus emptied. Passengers walked around or sat on the ground, spreading out blankets and relaxing in any shady patches they could find. Eventually, I plucked up enough courage to ask a group of young men about the problem. They laughed at my hesitant, mangled French, but one spoke English. He stood.

"Hello. My name is Moussa. Welcome in Algeria."

We shook hands, but he held onto my hand longer than one would do in England and led me around the bus to show me the broken fan belt. Feeling a little uncomfortable as he was still holding my hand, I reached in my pocket for a handkerchief and blew my nose. He grinned at me in a rather mischievous way. *Was he flirting with me?* I'd read about Arab men holding hands and how it just meant they were friends. I tried to regain my over-excited internal composure.

He was good-looking with short, curly hair and the shadow of a beard. Friendly and polite, he also had a roguish look—a seductive allure of adventure. Moussa told me he studied medicine at the University of Algiers and was visiting his family in Bou Saâda. I asked about the town, and he promised to show me everything and introduce me to all the girls.

"If we have car," Moussa lamented.

"What do you mean?"

"We pick up girls when they walk home after school. We arrange quick meeting. These girls are very willing."

"But isn't this dangerous?" I asked. "I've read stories of enraged fathers killing their daughters and—"

"Oh, do not worry. Algeria is socialist country. No one know. Ahhh, if only we have car."

I felt overwhelmed and embarrassed by his comment about the girls, not knowing how to respond. Moussa was charming, but I had no signposts to help me navigate situations like this.

Finally, the driver returned, replaced the fan belt, and we resumed our journey. We were behind schedule and did not arrive in Bou Saâda until late at night. The bus pulled in and stopped. One streetlamp illuminated the area, casting a pale light over the bus station, or more correctly, the side of the road where the bus had stopped. My fellow passengers retrieved their bags and departed up dark, unlit streets, but I felt disoriented. The town was quiet and empty, apart from a few people wrapped in cloaks sleeping on a sandy area in front of the bus station.

Moussa came up behind me and placed his hand on my shoulder, "They wait for bus to Algiers."

He stood right behind me, his body touching mine, making me feel uncomfortable by breaking the cultural space I was used to in a Western environment. I felt nervous and stuttered, "T-t-t-tell me, where is the nearest hotel?"

"Closed now. You stay with my house."

It was difficult to read the clues, he was coming across as very forward, but I wasn't sure how to react. I looked at the men lying on the hard ground. "I don't know. It's very kind of you, Moussa, but—"

"Come. Don't be British. You are guest. It is my honour."

He picked up my bags, and I followed him through the dark, winding streets. The air was warm and heavy with the scent of jasmine, emanating a sweet odour of the exotic. Sensing our presence, a few dogs barked. A warning? *Now I'm becoming paranoid. Relax*, I told myself. And in a way, it was pleasant to be here, in this unfamiliar town, beginning a new adventure. This is why I had come—to experience a new culture and be challenged by the unknown.

We entered a large house, imposing but showing signs of neglect. Moussa led me into the living room, gave me a couple of sheets, pointed at the couch, said, "Goodnight, Dave," and left me to sleep.

♦ ♦ ♦

I woke to early morning sunlight pouring through the lace curtains and the sound of doves crooning outside the window. I dozed, soothed by the sounds of nature.

Later, looking for a bathroom, I discovered a sink without water, a squat toilet, a blue plastic bucket, and a scoop. I reminded myself this was the desert. I had to adjust to a new reality.

I returned to the front room where I had slept and saw Moussa sitting on the couch, a breakfast tray on the table. He gestured towards it and told me to help myself. Hot strong coffee and a crusty French baguette with butter and jam made a pleasant filling breakfast. Moussa was gracious as a host, and we chatted while we ate.

"Did you sleep good, Dave?"

"Yes, Moussa, fine. Thanks." I felt at ease with the day and this friendly guy sitting opposite me. "Thank you for asking me here."

"Oh, it is nothing. You are my guest."

"Your English is excellent. Where did you learn it?"

"Thank you. I learn English at school and then study at England during summer."

"Where in England?" Spreading butter and honey on a chunk of bread, I looked up at Moussa and knew that we could become friends. Not just the small talk; it was the open and genuine way he expressed himself.

"Oxford. I have host family, Mr. and Mrs. Grosvenor, their son, John, and daughter, Joanne. They show me all over."

"That was kind."

"Yes. I learn of life in England. But must I ask—what happened with woman on bus? One of my friends see—no—saw you. You give her money."

"Yes, because they would have thrown her off the bus in a small village in the middle of nowhere."

"What did she do for money?"

"Nothing." I was shocked by a question I didn't want to answer.

"I told you the girls are . . ."

"I don't want to—"

"It's OK. It's normal. You are good-looking guy."

"Nothing happened. I didn't give her much—some change."

"Oh?" He smiled, looking straight at me.

I still wanted to be friends, but he'd managed to make me feel uncomfortable, so I reached for my coffee and, to change the subject, asked him about the town.

Later in the morning, he walked me to my designated school. There he introduced me to the *intendant*, the headmaster, who led me to a small cell-like room with a bed, a washbasin, a desk, and a chair. No electricity, but at least I had water.

The room above the empty school was small and depressing, with a view of a deserted schoolyard and a rocky, barren hill. Moussa had told me he had some urgent family business, but he would find me next time he came to Bou Saâda. My head was spinning; so much had happened in the last few days. *Had I done or said anything wrong? Moussa had seemed so genuine and polite.*

Feeling hungry, I left the school to explore the town, searching for a coffee shop or a restaurant. The central marketplace's noise and activity led me downhill to a café where I could sit, drink warm Orangina, and observe the flow of humanity.

I could taste the dust as it floated in the air and breathed in the pungent smell of animal dung. Heavily laden donkeys trotted past, led by stern, Old Testament-looking men with red-hennaed beards and long robes. Patched-up cars hooted and wove around the men and the sheep and goats that wandered onto the street. Peugeot 404 taxis circled the square, the drivers shouting destinations. When they stopped, the passengers hoisted their bags onto the roof rack, tied them down, and squeezed into what looked like an already packed car.

It was intoxicating. I had read so much about Algeria and this town, and now I was living and breathing it, watching little scenes play out in front of me.

There was so much I wanted to see in Bou Saâda. I'd read about Etienne Dinet, a French artist who'd converted to Islam and painted scenes of the Ouled Nail: A semi-nomadic Bedu tribe from the mountains around Bou Saâda. His paintings were exotic and attractive, giving a romantic vision of what it might have been like in the early 1900s. Another guidebook mentioned the *Ksar*, the old town. It described the narrow streets and small artisan shops where men carved knife handles and blacksmiths pounded the blades of the famous Bou Saâdi knives. There was an oasis of date palm trees in and around the Oued Bou Saâda, a usually dry river valley, but I'd read that it served as a watercourse when heavy rains deluged the area.

A French guidebook described Bou Saâda as the gateway to the Sahara. A little jewel of an oasis before the real challenges of the Sahara Desert began. I opened an English guide book and re-read the description of my town:

> An old French Foreign Legion fort perches on top of a small hill rising out of the town spread before it. The town crawls up the sides of one hillside and is cut by the green palmeraie and oued on the other. The palm trees lead toward the sandy plain and yellow dunes drift over to M'Sila and the Chott El Hodna.

THREE

Those first few weeks working and living in Algeria have all merged. There were times when I was getting by but suffering from culture shock. The other irritation was having to share with Seamus, a teacher in an all-girls school. They offered him an apartment, but as he would have to share with an Egyptian religious teacher, he refused and asked me. I agreed because the choice between living above the school or moving into a two-bedroom apartment was not too difficult to make.

The accommodation was bare in a building shared by other instructors. I bought a thin foam mattress to sleep on and a grey-blue blanket. Every morning, one of the French teachers woke early to start his Peugeot 404 diesel pickup. He left it running for at least ten minutes before revving it and driving off to school. The constant noise served as an unwelcome alarm clock.

In the afternoons, doors banged and kids ran noisily in the rooms above us. Their parents shouted, then slapped them, and the kids screamed. It was all very distressing and not the experience of the stimulating new culture I'd imagined. I had dreamed of living in a palmeraie in an old, peaceful, whitewashed Arab house, with cocks crowing in the morning and a few bleating goats. Instead, I was in this nightmare apartment with Seamus and neighbours from hell.

One day, Seamus showed me his tailor-made Algerian long "shirt" extending to his feet. It was white and made of fine cotton, a practical garment to wear in the summer to keep you cool. Westerners, including the French, rarely wore them unless they had converted to Islam. It was normally worn with long-legged cotton pants under the garment, Seamus insisted you didn't need to. He had walked downtown wearing his *djebella*. The sunlight shone through the light cotton, meaning his boxers and hairy legs were visible: not pretty!

"You're supposed to wear long cotton pants underneath. It's diaphanous."

"So what?"

"It doesn't look good on you. The people here are conservative and dressing like that isn't right."

"It doesn't matter."

At the time I had no idea, but that was the first strike against him.

A few days later, Seamus invited his tailor, Ahmed, to visit. He looked eighteen or nineteen and was handsome, with a dark complexion and black curly hair and, like many young men you see about town, wearing blue jeans and a white T-shirt.

We chatted in French about the usual things; life in Bou Saâda, his job, food. Then Seamus changed the subject and asked a personal question.

"Do you have a girlfriend, Ahmed?"

"No, you can't have girlfriends here," replied Ahmed, looking down at the floor.

Was he blushing? Hard to tell.

"Haven't you had any girlfriends, then?"

"No. I . . ." Ahmed looked down to reach for his tea glass.

Seamus laughed out loud. I felt embarrassed for him, but Seamus had his own peculiar way about him.

"Oh well, I've got something for you."

He laughed again and went into his bedroom. I shrugged, looking at Ahmed and wondering what Seamus was going to give him. He came out holding a magazine: *Penthouse.*

"Here. Take a look and enjoy yourself."

I was concerned about Seamus giving him the magazine, as pornographic magazines are banned in Algeria. It was as if he refused to adapt to Algeria's cultural, social, and religious norms. Seamus seemed very hard-headed. *Was he being deliberately provocative, but to what end?*

Strike Two.

♦ ♦ ♦

I taught English in a mixed school, but most schools were single-sex. A large number of English-speaking teachers were required because a political decision had been made to move Algeria away from relying only on French. English became the second international language to learn. The Ministry also stipulated that English-language teachers could only teach in English, and *Practice and Progress* had been selected as the book to use throughout Algeria.

One chapter talked about the Hindenburg Zeppelin that had burst into flames in 1937 attempting to dock in New Jersey. I tried to explain the word "Zeppelin," drawing one on the board. It ended up looking obscene, so I hastily erased it. I don't think the class understood what I had been trying to draw, but the boys decided to practice their own artistic skills a few days later.

During one lesson, I swung open the side blackboard to write on the back and revealed a chalk sketch of a penis. Embarrassed, especially for the girls, I hastily rubbed it out. The boys also drew the same image on the wooden chairs they wanted the girls to sit on. Unknowingly, I sat on one of these myself. The boys gasped, and then a few giggled, which caught on with the rest of the boys. I had no idea why they were laughing, until I stood up and looked down at the chair. I didn't make a fuss, and after a while the joke ran out of steam. No further penises appeared.

Seamus, however, taught at an all-girls school and had a somewhat mischievous bent. He was delighted with the idea of giving the Algerian youth an Irish accent.

One example was teaching the girls to count. "One, two, tree . . ." The counting followed by a great guffaw of laughter.

He couldn't stop talking, being one of those people who had to dominate and tell story after story. I rarely talked about my classes and let him continue. He had read his class the same chapter about the German Zeppelin. Of course, they had no idea what a Zeppelin was, so he had drawn one on the blackboard.

He sniggered, almost choking, and blurted out, "And you know? It looked like a giant penis. I couldn't stop laughing." He mentioned that his class of girls remained silent.

As there is no letter or "p" sound in Arabic, Pepsi is often pronounced as *Bebsi.* I later learned the Arabic slang word for penis is *zeb.* So, the word Zeppelin, or in Arabic, *zebblin,* must have sounded exceptionally crude. Drawing it didn't help.

Strike Three.

FOUR

I had a lot of time to think about the past. We only had to go to the school to teach lessons three days a week. On Wednesday and Fridays, I finished at one o'clock and I could leave.

I reflected on who and what I had left behind in the UK. The struggle of living in Algeria is what gave it character. We hadn't been paid yet, so I couldn't buy too many creature comforts, but I didn't mind. The scarcity made living challenging. It made you question the need for so many luxuries or choices of brands of soap. I didn't miss the pub or the shops. No, it was the lack of friends. The friendly banter and assured welcome, where I didn't have to explain myself. What I regretted most, though, was how my best friend Steve and I had parted.

Steve was tall and carefree in a way I could never be. His clothes gave him away, especially his Levi overalls: faded blue denim with a button-up top, sleeveless over a white T-shirt, and a Palestinian black-and-white checked scarf wound around his neck. His long red hair and scraggly beard completed the image. "Look at me. I'm different." As he walked down the street, people glanced and looked away. We were honked at by several drivers. He was gay and it was apparent.

He worked in the theatre and had a job as stage manager at the Manchester Palace. It was a grand name for a now sad, failing theatre, but it suited Steve as he could flounce off after the performance and do the rounds of the gay bars or attend parties where gay people gathered.

He wasn't attractive, but he'd enter a room and dominate it with loud laughs and inappropriate comments. Steve always wanted to control the conversation, to be applauded and admired. Was that part of his insecurity?

"Oh, Simon, look at you. All tarted up and nowhere to go. Peter, darling. Lilac? You do know lilac symbolizes innocence and purity. Not your colour at all, sweetie."

There was lots of sniggering at this, but Steve sashayed on, loving the attention. As the parties were full of friends and acquaintances, he'd be tolerated and allowed to get away with his flamboyant comments.

He'd been attacked a couple of times. Not surprising, in the seventies, when he flouted the social norms. Gay life then wasn't so easy. The police raided gay bars and clubs, and you could be beaten up in the streets for looking the "wrong" way at someone. The police could be brutal. You didn't bother reporting gay-bashing; you'd get locked up for turning up at the station. I knew Steve was into gay activism, and he'd sometimes talk at gay-lib meetings. He was out in a very open way.

Steve was more exciting than any of my other friends. He mocked authority and was a rebel, questioning society and its attitude toward gays. Being a bit of a loner, I had a few friends at school but wasn't particularly close to any of them. They were middle-class, straight-jacketed, and conventional. Nice guys. Pleasant, yet careful, knowing what jobs they would do after university: dentist, accountant, lawyer. I needed Steve. We fed exhilaration to one another.

Manchester University offered me a place to study Drama, while Steve got a theatre job. After getting my piece of paper, I became unemployable. My degree in Drama wasn't what employers wanted. I spent a few months promoting a circus in different towns around England, and then worked as a porter in a department store, picking up rubbish. I had a few minor roles in theatre, and once in a film as an extra. I had to stand around for hours for a three-minute shot, which became a second or two on screen. Steve had a full-time job, and he occasionally landed me an acting role. I was there because of him, a "kept man." Always short of money, I had to break free and become independent.

♦ ♦ ♦

After my failed attempt to get a teaching job in the UK, for which I am eternally grateful—the fates looked after me that day for sure—I applied desperately for a teaching job abroad. I knew I had to escape the rigor mortis of living in England. I was approaching twenty-four. What had I done with my life? I'd ticked the boxes, gone to university, and had a piece of paper. Now I had to decide what to do next. I wanted to be a writer and felt I needed experiences outside of my routine, everyday existence. I needed change, a challenge, and money.

The salary was decent, but I feared telling Steve. I kept putting it off, avoiding the inevitable. I booked my plane ticket and then, feeling nothing could stop me, I decided to tell him face-to-face what I was going to do. He lived in a rented room in a shared house occupied by theatre people, so he could be consoled if needed.

♦ ♦ ♦

It was a typical Manchester day in September: a leaden sky with heavy, dark clouds. I walked because it would have taken two buses and almost an hour rather than fifteen minutes through the park. But of course, I got caught in a sudden downpour of heavy lashing rain. A sudden burst of vengeful, blustering wind whipped the umbrella out of my hand, and it flew away. Soaked, I continued. The storm eased off, but a constant light pattering followed me all the way to Steve's house.

Dripping wet, cold, and miserable, I rang the doorbell, dreading what was going to follow.

"Hello, you. Oh, my little drowned rat. Come in."

I entered the hall, dripping and feeling like a betrayer. *How could I extract myself? This wasn't going to be pleasant.*

"Let's get those clothes off you. We can warm you up in a hot bath."

It was that expectation, that lure, I knew I had to resist.

"No. Look, I've got to say something."

Steve continued in a pleasant, welcoming voice as if he hadn't heard me. "I didn't know you were coming. Why didn't you let me know?"

"I've called you a few times, but you never seem to be in." I forced a smile.

"Well, I'm out having fun. Remember fun?"

He was getting at me, as we hadn't been out clubbing in a few weeks. I had tired of the same loud dance music, smoke-filled rooms with guys desperately wanting to score.

"Well," he said, "you do look cute. As wet as you are, I could ravish you right here on the stairs."

Steve was deliberately being outrageous. It was all a joke with Steve. Stevie? Isn't that what he preferred now?

"Look Sss . . . Stevie," I stuttered, "I came to tell you . . . I'm going away. I've . . ."

"What do you mean you're going away? Another job? Super."

"I w-w-w-w-w . . ." Nerves and fear made me stutter. I tried to speak again. "I w-w-w-w . . ."

Steve laughed. It made me determined. I stamped my foot to clear the speech I'd rehearsed, and it came out in a gush.

"I've got a job: Teaching in Algeria. Leaving in a few days."

His look of hurt and dismay stopped me. His face fell as he looked at me.

"You can't leave. What about me?"

"Why is it always about you? I need the money. I can't go on doing crappy little roles, penniless, living in a flea-ridden garret, or relying on you to get me an insignificant part at the theatre."

"You selfish prick. I stick my neck out getting you those 'insignificant parts,' as you call them."

"I'm sorry, I didn't mean it like that. It's just … I have to do something with my life. Knowing you has been great, but . . ."

His face stern, Steve spat out in a fury I'd never heard before, "So that's it—is it? We're finished?"

I grabbed the door and rushed out. Walking away, I heard him spit out one last word. "Bastard."

The door slammed behind me.

FIVE

Sometimes, when walking the streets of Bou Saâda, everything seemed perfect. Early in the morning, I wandered down to the market. There I could handle the tomatoes, onions, carrots, and garlic, breathe in the fresh, tempting aroma of vegetables dug from the earth and taste the sweet purple grapes plucked from the vine a few hours ago.

Later, I climbed Kardada, a mountain of barren, shattered, sharp rocks, a few clumps of grass, and thorny bushes. I stepped carefully to avoid a shiny, black beetle laboriously snub-nosing its way across the sunbaked rocks. The view from the top was magnificent. I called it Eagle Point as it resembled an eagle's aerie, with a superb overview of the almost empty valley below. Sounds carried: a truck rumbling and a muezzin calling. A couple of crows flew past, their feathers rustling. Sand martins dived, flashing past me, chasing insects, their wing beats urgent and fast.

Standing and looking over this stupendous view, I felt powerful and imagined myself soaring, circling in the currents of rising air and the lord of all I surveyed.

The following week of teaching loomed, and the demands of life imposed its humdrum demands. I clambered down the mountain to go shopping.

The supermarket was a sad place full of empty, forlorn shelves, waiting for the delivery of whatever item would arrive from the North. There were exercise books and pens and all the usual school apparatus, but not any variety or quality. Cans of jam, tomato paste, and green beans stocked the food section. Sometimes, you would find a glut of butter or Edam cheese. The hard-to-obtain item led to a mad scramble to acquire as much as possible before it disappeared. Many customers were *commerçants,* intent on buying large quantities to sell as a luxury item when the supply was exhausted.

I wanted to buy a bottle of wine. Rows of shining bottles had been there for the last few weeks, but today I discovered Fanta had replaced the wine. People scrabbled and fought for the bottles. But without a fridge, I would have to drink it warm. Still, it was better than the sickly-sweet bottles of Gazooz: an occasionally fizzy drink rather like an Algerian version of Fanta. Gazooz came in three different colours rather than flavours and was presented in chipped, opaque bottles. Today, people pushed and shoved around the shelves and shouted at the cashier to attract his attention rather than queueing.

"Asma, Mohammed. Asma." (Listen, Mohammed. Listen.)

While standing waiting to pay, a hand patted me on the shoulder. "Dave, I did not see you for some time. How are you?"

"Moussa. It's great to see you. I'm fine. How are you? Back from university for a holiday?"

"No. Weekend. Let's go for drink."

He suggested we go over to Al Caïd Hotel and told me it was a great place to pick up French or Australian girls. "It is tourist stop on the Sahara tour. We can meet. If we have car, we can take them for drive and back in my house."

"I can't, man. I'm a teacher here. I can't risk it, and I don't have any money to buy a car—we haven't been paid yet."

The hotel was modern and impressive, with white exterior walls and a beautiful shady garden where birds sang and flowers bloomed. A paradise in contrast to the dusty streets outside the confines of the hotel. In the evening, you could smell the tiny white jasmine flowers wafting their scent into the air, heady and sensual. Jasmine always reminded me of my arrival, my first night in this town—always a wonderful feeling.

That evening, though, the hotel was empty, apart from a few Arab businessmen, so Moussa asked if I wanted to go to the local hammam. These were Arab-style bathhouses—many of the older houses didn't have adequate hot water or indoor bathrooms. As Moussa told me, it was also traditional: a place to meet friends and chat about life away from the house.

In our building, we had an allowance of water for about an hour a day, if we were lucky. It usually came at five in the morning, with a gurgling then sudden gushing of water through the taps, and we let it fill the small sit-down bathtub. I hadn't had a hot bath since arriving but lacked the nerve to go to a hammam alone. I was reluctant, as a neophyte, to enter what I knew to be a private, all-male preserve, which I felt had its own modes of ritual. However, as none of the ex-pat French or British I knew had been, it held an intriguing forbidden-fruit temptation. I knew of a little run-down bathhouse in the old part of town. An unpaved street led to a sunken doorway with five steps to what must have been the old town's previous level. It looked rather unappealing, but that was the hammam we went to.

"Yes, Dave, old, but inside good. You will like."

Moussa paid, and the older man behind the counter gave him a couple of bars of soap and two pieces of folded cotton cloths. We descended four worn steps to a changing room. Moussa told me to watch what he did. He took off his shirt, so I did the same. Then I started to take off my jeans, as you might do in a men's changing room in the UK. There was an intake of breath from one of the men lying under a towel on my right.

Moussa grabbed my hand, stopped me, and wrapped a piece of material, like a sarong, around my waist. He whispered, "Remember. Watch me first."

He wrapped the sarong around his waist, then took off his trousers and pants. I did the same, a little embarrassed.

On entering the large central area, the humidity hit you like a fist to the stomach. It was gloomy, with the only light filtering in from four windows in the high domed roof. Steam wafted around the circular room. In a few minutes, sweat beaded on my forehead then trickled into my eyes.

The thick stones of the building shielded us from the bustle of the town, and inside, sounds were deadened. Then, without warning, pipes rattled, and streams of steaming hot water gushed and squealed into basins but just as suddenly stopped, followed by an eerie silence that embalmed the room.

A few men lay on stone benches, occasionally sitting up and pouring buckets of water over themselves. We sat, letting the heat open our pores and release the sweat and dirt. Finally, a boy beckoned to us. Moussa acknowledged him and told me, "This boy, Hakim. He work here. I pay him wash us."

Sitting on heavy stone benches, we soaped ourselves then involuntarily inhaled as Hakim poured buckets of hot water over us. After rinsing, Moussa lay down. I watched, dismayed, as this fifteen-year-old boy scrubbed him with a hand cloth, a kind of abrasive mitten. I flinched. In a few minutes, I was going to have my skin rubbed raw with this medieval-looking form of torture.

Hakim started by scrubbing my back and chest. I could feel the scratching as he worked his way down my arm. All my nerves were on alert, but it wasn't painful, more of a vigorous rubbing, and when scrub-boy stopped, I felt a flush of relief. Hakim worked on my hands, paying particular attention to my fingers, which he cracked, and then my legs and feet. I could feel the layers of dead skin sloughing off, like a snake shedding its old skin. It was not as painful as I had feared and, in fact, was strangely pleasant.

Later, recovering from the scrubbing, sweating, and buckets of hot water, we returned to the dressing room and laid down. An older man put towels over us while we rested. Relaxing, the freshness and renewal felt spiritual. Drifting into this state of bliss, I mused about Arab tradition, and stress-free, my bond of friendship with Moussa strengthened.

He invited me over to his place, informing me that his parents had gone to Oran for the weekend. He wanted to show me his collection of 45s—mostly Beatles records from the 60s. We listened, singing some songs and even dancing a little. "Help" was one of his favorites. He uncorked a bottle of wine. It was Friday night.

"Je suis beau, non?" He laughed at my look of surprise. I had heard this in the street as cocky youths passed the odd foreign woman brave enough to venture out alone. Thinking I didn't understand, he switched to English. "You think I am sexy?" he asked, laughing.

"Yeah, you're very handsome, with beautiful, shining brown eyes. I'm sure the girls swoon when they see you."

"What is swoon mean?"

"Oh, you know, like fainting because you are so . . ."

"So sexy. Yes, I know, beautiful brown eyes. I know. You swoon when you see me?"

I laughed. "Moussa, I like you, but . . ."

"But what? Here are no girls. We are alone. We could have fun."

"You know, you're over-sexed. That's all you think about."

But he was charming. His deep brown eyes, sparkling with the joy of life, penetrated my very being. He had a sexual magnetism, and his sensuality and charm drew me into his embrace.

He laughed in delight, and I was lost. We kissed, and the hair on the back of my neck tingled. All my pent-up desire and sexual frustrations welled up in me. We clawed at each other's clothes, as the acute need for sex possessed us.

SIX

Hugh is an English eccentric, rather like a remnant from the days of Empire, although he'd hate me to say that, and of course, the British never occupied Algeria. He's a small, thin, well-dressed man in his mid-forties. I first encountered him in the dusty streets of the old town of Bou Saâda, and upon discovering I was English, he immediately invited me to his house.

"Do come for tea."

We walked to his place in the old quarter. Here, the streets are dried mud and sand and flow down toward the Oued Maïtar: the dry river valley, channeling floodwater to the not-so-distant desert sands. A few mopeds wove past, ridden by devil-may-care youths, their bikes belching and rattling. Older men padded quietly back from the market carrying blue plastic bags with carrot leaves or tomatoes bulging out and occasionally an upside-down squawking chicken. The area had character, and it was, of course, cheaper than the newer areas near the central market. There, heavily laden Peugeot 404 pickups maneuvered their way past donkey carts and pedestrians, blasting at everything in their path.

The houses in the old quarter were mostly stone, with white-painted plaster peeling off the walls. They were not kept up and neat like middle-class British houses, but they were impressive. Many of them had a large, arched stone entrance with a heavy, fitted wooden door, and inset in this, like a church door, a smaller door that opened inwards. Hugh's was an incredible pastel blue, flaking like the walls but stately. His house, located above the steep sides of the oued, was in a favoured spot, I imagined. He led the way down the cool corridor, away from the intense, blazing sun.

He chuckled. "Haven't stopped all day today."

We entered his main living room, a large bright room with a patio leading to his dusty but neatly swept garden overlooking the dry valley and waving palm trees. I noticed the *Observer* newspaper, folded to the crossword, lying on a chair, and a young Arab boy sitting on a mattress against the wall. Hugh didn't speak to him or introduce me. The boy, who looked sixteen and was wearing dirty jeans and an off-white T-shirt, got up and disappeared into another room.

After a while, the young, sullen lad—who I decided must be the houseboy—re-entered the room. He resembled the scores of kids you see running around the streets, not begging but pestering and cheekily seeing what they could get away with. I decided to call him "Village Boy" with his air of unkemptness: curly, short-cropped hair and a spotty face. Village Boy brought in a tray with a teapot, the cups and saucers carefully arranged. He put it down on a small side table next to Hugh with a look of utmost concentration. I could almost hear the sigh of relief, as nothing had been broken or spilled. I guessed Hugh was training him in the arts of being a server.

"Would you like some tea?" asked Hugh. He didn't acknowledge Village Boy.

"Yes, please."

"Milk?"

"A little. Thank you."

"Earl Grey? I have a friend in London send it over in a little food parcel, like the Red Cross." Hugh laughed softly but also, I thought, a little smugly.

Earl Grey was quite a delicacy here in this little town on the edge of the Sahara. I'd been here for two months and hadn't seen any kind of British tea, let alone Earl Grey.

He carefully poured the tea through a strainer into delicate china cups. As we drank, he sat with a straight back, one leg resting neatly across his other knee. We talked about books. I noticed he had an extensive library pushed up against the walls: *French Country Cooking* nestling against Kafka's *The Castle*. This plethora of books was a precious find in Algeria, but he never offered to lend any. He showed me his name written on the flyleaf of every book.

Hugh told me he had been in Algeria for almost seven years but had little social contact with the French. As a joke, he had tacked a hand-drawn map of Europe onto the wall. Spain had become an island, and a vast sea submerged France under the English Channel, the Atlantic Ocean, and the Mediterranean Sea. It prompted me to ask an innocent enough question, "Don't you like the French?"

He gave a slight shudder and chuckled, shaking his head. "They always take so long over their meals, and they talk incessantly."

I later learned Hugh spoke French perfectly, and four of his colleagues at the hotel training school where he taught were French, but it's one of the little jokes we "British" have.

I noticed postcards of naked Greek Gods pinned to the walls and a small statue of a satyr sporting an enormous phallus placed prominently on his writing desk. On the opposite wall: a Lowry print of Oldham factories and terraced houses populated with lonely stick-like people tramping the streets, his idiosyncratic map of Europe, and a temperature chart plotting the fluctuations daily over the year. I asked him, perhaps too bluntly, why he liked living in Bou Saâda. Maybe it's because I needed confirmation to help me understand why I was here. He answered directly and without thinking about it.

"I'm like a piece of driftwood cast upon the shore. It's the light, the sun's warmth, the freshness and purity of the air, and the aesthetic beauty of the desert."

Later, I gleaned another reason. Hugh showed me his photo album. I glanced over these images of Hugh's life, Hugh with his mother, and others of youths standing self-consciously in front of dunes, palm trees, or by the oued.

"Oh, those? Some of my students from the hotel school. Oh, that's Mohammed. Before he came to our school, he'd never left that dirty excuse for a village, Ain Djelfa. It was quite a job to refine him, I can tell you."

He mentioned them a little offhandedly, but I assumed he had a never-ending supply of young men to befriend and "refine."

After about ten minutes or so, Village Boy got up to leave, but Hugh barely noticed.

"Oh! You're going then. Goodbye. *Au revoir*," he said to the disappearing Algerian's back. Then turning to me, "More tea?"

As we discussed *Brideshead Revisited* and Evelyn Waugh's Catholicism, another kid walked in and threw himself down on the rolled-up mattress. Hugh ignored him, then said something facetious to me in French about his annoying habits, mainly when this "boy" played the radio too loud. The youth was impressive in a rough, feral way but smelt of goats and wood smoke. He shrugged, took a flute from his pocket, and played it instead. Hugh chatted on. After a while, Goat-Boy left, or so I thought, but I heard a radio playing softly in the bedroom as I left. I surmised he was waiting for Hugh to start his lessons.

A few days later, amongst the noise and bustle of the vegetable market and fondling misshapen tomatoes that burst with succulent freshness once bitten, I saw Hugh across the stall from me.

Easy to recognize, Hugh always wore a tie and insisted on his students doing the same, claiming it a rule of the establishment. But it fits with the last vestiges of colonialism. Hugh dressed well. Not in a dandy or ostentatious manner, but—well, as an Englishman. He looked different as he wove his way through the sellers, passing the wandering, lingering older men in dirty burnooses and the strutting young men in tight, buttock-hugging jeans.

"Oh, hello. Look, can't stop now. Must dash. I've got a class at eleven. All right, are you? Good. Good. Well, look, I must pop up and visit you sometime this week."

"Yes, of course, do," I said, knowing full well he had no intention of doing so.

He's always in a hurry and doesn't like idle chatter. In Bou Saâda, faucets only work for an hour or so, then they gurgle and dry up, so I didn't want to overdo the visits as it would be too much for both of us.

SEVEN

Elizabeth, a new teacher, arrived in October, a few weeks later than the rest of us. She was twenty-four and straight out of teacher training college. She had the apartment next door, and we spent quite a few evenings drinking and chatting, but mostly talking about England and our reasons for coming to Algeria. We both wanted to justify our coming to Algeria, but the "why" had become hard to define. Though, a desire to escape is what we had in common.

Liz echoed my own feelings. "I hadn't wanted to teach in the UK, as I felt it would be too dreary. The only reason I had taken up teaching in the first place was to get a job abroad and travel, getting as much experience as I could."

Her desire to leave the UK was similar to mine, but she came from a very different background. She had lived all her life in a strict, Christian, middle-class atmosphere in Colchester: a little town north of London in Essex. I told her I came from the northeast of England and for fun did my Geordie accent; "U arreet, pet?"

She looked a little flustered, understanding, but not sure what to say. She continued, "I've never been that far north. I'd always lived at home with my parents, even going to Essex Uni. They controlled my life, so I hadn't lived. Algeria gave me the chance to escape the safety blanket cocooning me."

"Yes, I know." *Should I move closer?* I refilled her glass, and she took a long gulp.

"This is so satisfying." She giggled. "I do enjoy talking to you. I want to confess everything—to let it all out. I've never talked like this before. Here, I feel free. You know I'm quite shy and lonely here. I can't speak much French and no Arabic. I'm reliant on the company of other English speakers."

"It's the same for most of us. Don't let it worry you. You'll settle down," I said to comfort her. I opened a second bottle and filled her glass.

She tossed her head, and her long hair cascaded down her shoulders.

"You are beautiful," I said, "with your golden hair falling down your back." *Oh, Christ,* I thought. *That must be the worst pickup line ever. Get a grip, Dave.*

She laughed and continued, "I should tell you it didn't work out with a boyfriend in uni. I come from a very religious family, and I insisted he could only touch me above the waist."

"Right. I know what you mean." I remembered a girl I'd known at school. Heavy petting but no touching the nether regions. She went to church as well, so I knew it wouldn't be appropriate to tell her.

"Then he asked me to have sex with him on his twenty-first birthday. I told him 'No.' I said something like, 'If that's what you want, we might as well end it here.'"

A warning? She's a virgin? I filled her glass again and poured some for myself.

She continued her story. "I still remember the relief those words gave me, but in my last year, I was a friendless virgin. Another reason Algeria appealed. I wanted to run away and start the life of my dreams—the French Foreign Legion, Beau Geste, romance."

Should I make a move, hold her hand, kiss her neck? She was getting quite tipsy. I could smell her perfume, Estée Lauder:

subtle but heady. It made me fantasize, as I could feel the warmth of her body close to mine.

"You know Beau, don't you? He invited me over. I love his place."

"Do you like him because he is French and sexy?" *Why did I say that?*

Beau worked as an English teacher at a middle school in Bou Saâda. He's thirty-something, clean-shaven with blond, shoulder-length, carefully tousled hair. Beau was one of the French *coopérants* doing two years teaching in an ex-French colony instead of a year of military service. Appealing and delightful, he also had a look of sly craftiness, an air of "don't totally trust this man," or "don't believe what you see is what you get." But I envied his debonair attraction only a Frenchman can pull off. He had a sexual magnetism that pulled people into his orbit, and I wondered if he liked guys.

Beau spoke perfect English and loved to entertain both French and British expats. His living room had character with comfortable mattresses covered with printed fabrics in dark red and blue. Bedouin carpets lay scattered over the floor along with a low glass-topped coffee table, copper coffee pots, rose de sables, a crystallized rock formation, and a large, hefty slice of fossilized wood. It was a pleasant place to lounge around in, read a book, and gossip about people.

"I went to Beau's place last weekend, you know. We had fun. A few of the French teachers and Seamus were there. God, I can't stand him. He's so arrogant." She giggled. "I never would have said that back home."

"You know what I saw in his bedroom?" I asked her in a catty way, trying to influence her thoughts about Beau. "Returning from the bathroom, I peeked into his room and hanging on the wall I saw a couple of those mass-produced pictures supposed to be cute but also risqué."

She raised her eyebrows. *Right,* I thought, *I'd got a bite. Now to reel her in.*

"In one, a naked boy is standing in front of a blazing fire. He is turning around to look at you, and you can see his fat little bottom and his sweet smiling face. On the other wall, a picture of another naked boy peeing into a pot holding his little piddler. He was smiling and looking around, with his two rounded buttocks showing. Not in the best possible taste."

She shuddered, and I laughed. But she dismissed my attempt to smear Beau, "Oh, they sound sweet. He's having a party next weekend to celebrate being paid. Did you know? Yes? Well, we'll have to go, sing songs, and tell lots of stories."

"Yeah, sounds like fun. We can go together."

"OK. Now I do think it's time I went. We've got school in the morning. Thank you so much for listening to me. Goodnight, Dave." Without saying anything more, she got up and returned to her place next door.

Did she know I wanted to kiss her? Had Liz even registered me?

The British teachers decided to have dinner in a new restaurant in town and then go to Beau's party. It was a fantastic meal: lamb kebabs, delicious white wine, crusty fresh baguette, and masses of couscous. We ate like gluttons and then gossiped about the other teachers while eating sweet dates and tangerines.

Interestingly, Algeria had a somewhat schizophrenic attitude toward alcohol. Of course, it is banned in Islam, but Algeria had been a major wine-growing region during the French occupation. Then after the revolution, many vineyards were bulldozed for food production. However, the country still has a sizeable commercial wine and beer industry. You could discreetly buy bottles in a ware-house-type building at the edge of town and order wine or beer in the larger hotels and restaurants. As long as you were discreet about it, you could buy it.

We arrived at Beau's place carrying bottles of wine and beer we'd bought earlier and joined the already lively party. Beau was playing his guitar, and everyone was drinking and chatting, enjoying the evening. Later, I noticed some of the younger French teachers left quietly, and Seamus went out with them.

I asked Liz if she wanted to walk home with me, but she said Beau had offered to drive her back later. That's when I regretted not having a car and understood Moussa's comments about the advantages of being able to drive.

The next day, I learned from Seamus it had been quite a drinking session with some of the French teachers and a few young Algerians. Seamus told me about some of the political topics that were discussed in the drunken hours of the early morning. Seamus mentioned they had talked about Boumédiène, the President of Algeria, dying, and speculating that he was already dead. The French community talked about it, but the government-controlled news media didn't want anyone to know until a successor had been chosen.

Seamus proudly stated he hadn't returned until early in the morning. He had fallen asleep in his room, not waking until eleven with someone banging on the door.

"I struggled out of bed to answer the door. Mokhtar, one of the *surveillants,* you know, those discipline freaks, said something like, 'Mr. Breedon, are you all right? We miss you at school.' I told him, 'I'm feeling terrible. Stomach—something I ate. Couldn't stop going to the toilet. I'll be all right tomorrow.' 'OK,' he said. 'I tell *proviseur*.'"

Of course, he knew Seamus wasn't sick. The fumes on his breath were enough.

Strike four.

EIGHT

Saturday evening, five of us went out for dinner at El Caïd hotel, and then Seamus, Liz, and I returned to my place to open a second bottle of wine. We talked about our students and compared life in Algeria with the UK. But later, feeling juiced up with that false, alcohol-infused confidence, Seamus annoyed Liz by talking about how successful he'd been with Agnes, Liz's flatmate.

"Oh yes," said Seamus, "She was up for it. I'm telling you. Couldn't stop her. All over me. I think she liked the Irish accent." Followed by a roar of laughter.

"Oh, shut up," Liz shot back. "Agnes is one of the nicest girls I've ever met. She'd never have anything to do with you. You're an arrogant, puffed-up bore."

Seamus smirked with a knowing shake of his head, and his whole demeanor changed. "Oh, got you now. I know all about you and Beau." Seamus looked at Liz with a hostility and coldness that I hadn't seen in him before.

"What are you talking about, you conceited fool?" Liz was angry and drunk but also very aggressive. She shouted, "Who the hell do you think you are?"

Seamus wasn't flustered. In fact, he looked unsympathetic and arrogant. "Oh, yes. The French are all talking about it. The uptight, haughty English girl deflowered is what I heard."

"What?" I could see Liz's blood draining from her face.

Seamus continued in his irritating, supercilious way. "Beau made a bet with the Frenchies that he could seduce you. He put two thousand dinars on it, and he won." Seamus laughed again—a real nasty laugh.

I could see the shock and embarrassment on Liz's face. She jumped up and ran back to her flat, haunted by Seamus' lewd, gleeful laughter.

I couldn't speak to Seamus—couldn't look at him—hating him for what he had said. I endured a long, sleepless night, agonizing about what had happened to Liz and wondering how I could comfort her and what I could say to help her recover from the shame.

The whole week I tried knocking on her door, but she either didn't answer or shouted an angry, "Go away." Asking around, I found out that after teaching, she rushed home. However, on Friday, she opened the door.

"Hi Liz, how are you?" I asked delicately. "I haven't seen you for a few days."

She shrugged.

"Do you want to go for a walk? I thought you might like to climb Kardada and get out of the flat for a while." I had recovered from the fact that Beau had seduced her. It didn't rankle, feeling she was better as a friend—the only real friend I had here.

We climbed the hill, scrambling over rocks and up to the plateau. I wanted to take her to my special place: Eagle Point. Being on top of the world gave me the strength to continue during bleak and hard times. I wanted Liz to feel the same intensity.

Standing on the edge of the cliff face and looking down at the world stretched out before us was exhilarating. We embraced the wind, buffeted by the updraft. Then we sat on the rocks, our feet dangling over the chasm beneath us. Looking down at the view gave Liz the confidence to talk to me.

"It was a lovely night, very romantic. He lit candles and put on a cassette of Idir playing guitar, his voice rising and falling—soft, melodious music. Beau poured me another glass of wine. I floated and luxuriated in another body."

She stopped and looked at the barren hills and the line of the river, glinting and winding its way along the valley floor.

"It's beautiful here." I said, "I feel free and powerful."

She took a deep breath. "Yes, I know what you mean."

Sitting in silence, we felt comfortable in each other's presence.

"Of course," she continued in a faint, hesitant voice, "what happened was inevitable. He was so attractive and romantic—his blond hair, the music, the soft lights. His light, wandering hands electrified me, and I fell in love with him."

She paused. I was her confidant—her best friend. She needed release from the thoughts that had been raging around her head all week. The drama and remoteness of the setting gave her the strength to expose her inner feelings.

"He seduced me, and I changed to a 'before' me and an 'after' me. Innocence—and my carefully guarded virginity—lost." Her voice betrayed a sense of desolation and despair.

"I can't understand why he did it for a bet. I mean, it's so callous, so . . ." I searched for another word.

Liz sat and looked out at the vast expanse of barren hills and the sparkling twist of silver winding its way east. The updraft cooled us, and for a few seconds I imagined launching myself into the emptiness and swooping down to the river glinting below. Then, realizing Liz might feel the same, I grabbed her, and we shuffled further back until we were away from the edge of oblivion. Sitting on the rock ledge with our backs against another mass of solid rock, I felt secure. The dizziness and desire to jump lessened, and I put my arm around Liz to let her know I cared about her.

She looked a little dazed but continued, "Going into class, it's like another me. This other being going through the motions. Beau's act of betrayal has left me feeling . . . lost."

Liz started shaking. I held her, comforting her, becoming more like a brother. "It's OK to cry." I wanted to be her pillar of strength, to give her something to cling to. Being held gave her the confidence to let go. Liz sobbed, letting her feelings of betrayal and humiliation bubble out.

"No. No. I'm not going to let him destroy me." Liz wiped her face with her sleeve. I passed her my flask of water, and she sipped a little. Recovering, and with a determination that startled me, she announced, "He has to pay. Do you understand?" Her eyes blazed with a hardness and determination that I had never seen before.

"Yes, I'm with you."

"I can't stop thinking of what Seamus said. All the French know?" The anger in her voice built as if an alternate version of Liz had emerged.

"Beau took a bet that he could seduce me? I hate Seamus for the way he told me. The glee in his voice. The desire to shame me. That's unforgivable. And Beau? The arrogant bastard. My virginity is worth a couple of thousand dinars? He made a bet? As God is my witness, I want revenge."

I'd never heard anyone say anything like that before, but I could see Liz was deadly serious. It was doubly insulting because you could not change the Algerian dinar into foreign currency unless you used the black market, so it only had value inside Algeria. We all had more than enough dinars. I asked quietly, "What will you do?"

"Wipe that arrogant smirk off Seamus' face and get Beau. They can't treat me like this." She stood, and I had to scramble to stand in front of her to match her newly found determination. "Will you help?"

An ultimatum I couldn't refuse. Her anger felt real and I could tell she was determined. I understood why she needed me, and I was up for it. I replied quickly, "Yes, of course. But remember: Revenge is a dish best served cold."

We didn't realize then, but the ramifications of her desire for revenge changed our lives irrevocably.

NINE

During those first few months in Algeria, I thought a lot about Steve, missing his close friendship and biting humour. The scene of our parting kept replaying in my head, magnified by feeling homesick and longing for a past I had vowed to forget. I had taken a road forward, but now, apart from Liz, I didn't have a soulmate. Being lonely, I replayed events, creating different endings.

My letter contained words of apology, regret, and my feelings for Steve. Telling him how I hadn't appreciated our relationship. But in trying to appease him, I created a fantasy of how our friendship had been. This chocolate-box image erased all the darker aspects.

I had made plans to fly back to the UK during the winter holiday and buy a left-hand drive car in London, so I asked if we could meet in Manchester. As a kind of reunion, I mentioned taking a break and coming back with me to Bou Saâda and the Sahara.

◆ ◆ ◆

I arrived in Manchester late in the evening. It was pouring. The roads were slick from water gushing along the streets and shiny with the reflected glare of headlights from the surge of traffic.

47

It looked and felt exciting at first, but on reflection, England lacked the vibrancy and colour of Algeria. It was cold and bleak in the rain, and even though I wanted to see Steve, I needed to return to the desert to have a peaceful, meaningful life. I ran around the train station looking for a phone box. I'd done the apology bit, and Steve had replied, saying it was OK. Still, I wasn't totally sure as he could be very mercurial. I persuaded myself that as we were mates, catching up could be fun. Then, nervous as hell, I dialed his number.

"Steve? Hi, it's me. I'm back." *What is wrong with me? I sound like a seventeen-year-old kid.*

"So, it's you, you bastard," Steve said in a friendly, non-hostile way. I breathed a sigh of relief. "Are you coming over?"

"Yes, I'd like to."

I took a taxi from the station and gave the driver the address on Canal Street: right in the heart of gay Manchester. We drove past rows and rows of terraced, red-brick houses with back alleys. The taxi pulled up at Steve's place. It was the same as all the other houses, and I felt depressed and almost claustrophobic. I'd come from a land of light with the refreshing odours of desert flowers after a brief rainstorm to a real-life Lowry depiction of the remnants of an industrial wasteland. A wave of nausea washed over me, and I remembered the last time I had stood outside a door in the rain to tell him about leaving for Algeria. Now here I was, repeating the scene again. A different door with different news, but I still feared his reaction. Shivering, with trepidation, I rang the doorbell. Before I could have walked away, now I was committed.

"Hi, Steve."

"Hi, sweetie. Come on in. Get out of the rain. You look great."

"Thanks. You don't look too bad yourself."

Steve led me up the stairs, turning to let me into his flat and patting my bottom as I went through the door. Inside, he pressed up against me, pushing me back against the wall, and we kissed. I submitted to his hands running over me and dragging off my clothes. He grabbed my crotch, fondling me.

"I've wanted this for so long," he said in a dirty, familiar, aggressive voice as if punishing me for how I had left him.

The next day, we went to the theatre to have lunch in the foyer. Steve, in his element, acted over-the-top gay, showing me off to his friends. I felt like a prize bull paraded as an exhibit. *Why had I wanted to see him again? Was I so lonely in Algeria? Was I so desperate to need this—to be controlled and possessed?*

◆ ◆ ◆

But, away from his theatre people, he was calmer, and we bonded in those few days driving through France. December before Christmas was an atmospheric but quiet time to be travelling. We decided to visit the First World War battlefields, as Steve wanted to see where his grandfather had fought. We drove South through Picardy and visited the war memorials and battlefield sites of the Somme. Overcast, grey, cold, and wet, the weather created a solemn, appropriate atmosphere as the early morning mist drifted like gun smoke across the fields. Visiting this area helped us understand the misery and hardships the soldiers in the trenches must have gone through.

We stopped in Senlis and found an old nineteenth-century hotel: *L'Hôtel du Nord*. A faded grand hotel with high ceilings and a fusty wood-panelled dining room. Linen-covered tables laden with cutlery and glasses had been set as if for a dinner party, and an air of neglect and melancholy haunted the room.

An elderly grey-haired waiter served the set meal, French onion soup followed by *steak frites* and *crème caramel*. He shuffled between the serving hatch and our table. Apart from asking us for our orders and if we wanted wine, he didn't speak to us, even though we were the only diners. Black and white photographs of deserted streets and smashed houses, after being shelled by the Germans during the war, lined the walls. The silence, apart from the scraping of our cutlery on the heavy china plates, added to the faded glory and ghost-like atmosphere. A sense of melancholy haunted the room, and the whole experience somersaulted us back in time.

We imagined ourselves as British army officers, on leave from the front. Robert Graves and Siegfried Sassoon could have stayed in a hotel very much like this one. We talked about their heroism and Sassoon's gesture of throwing his Military Cross for valor into the River Mersey to protest the war. The First World War had been called "The war to end all wars," but it didn't. Even though it was so brutal, we could not even begin to comprehend the horror of it.

TEN

Late December, 1978

The day Steve and I arrived in Bou Saâda, we ran into Hugh. After the introductions, Hugh invited us to a party at his house with some other English-speaking expats.

"You must come. It's a welcome back, and I'm having some of the French as well."

He shuddered theatrically. "Well, I'm only asking them as a show of European solidarity, you know what I mean? Oh, and a few Algerians—some of my friends, and you know Moussa, don't you?"

I nodded.

"Right. I invited him, too. You know, a mix of Europeans and Arabs."

"How do you know Moussa?" I asked, a little puzzled.

"Oh, I don't know. I met him at the hammam, I think. He's quite a charmer." Hugh simpered and raised his eyebrows at the same time. "Anyway, do come and bring your friend. It'll be fun. Look, can't stop now. Got so much to do."

We walked to the main square, and I saw some of the French teachers sitting at an outdoor table at the popular *Café de la Jeunesse*. I knew them: single young men teaching in former French colonies instead of doing military service. I stopped to

51

greet them and shook hands with everyone, *"Bonjour"* and *"Ça va?"* all around. They introduced me to Susan, a new arrival—an American, so we chatted in English.

A little later, she asked me, "Where did you say you were going?"

"Oh, we're heading down to Ghardaïa. Steve here has taken a few days off work and is flying back to the UK just before school starts. Is everything going well for you?"

"No, not really. I've just arrived and have nowhere to stay. The school authorities won't give me an apartment until term starts."

"Typical. It depends on the school, I think. Never mind, stay at my place. My flatmate hasn't arrived yet and I'm leaving tomorrow with Steve, so the place will be empty."

"Really?"

"Yeah, why not? Come over tonight if you like. We'll be leaving early."

"Thank you."

"Oh yeah, we've been invited to a friend's house tonight. Come to the party first, and then we can go back to my place."

We all had a fantastic time, with lots of talking and bottles of the best Algerian red wine: Cuvée du Président. We lay on Bedouin hand-woven carpets, whispering and listening to an Algerian flute-playing youth creating haunting music that floated into the bright, star-speckled sky. A cedar-scented wood fire beside us crackled and spat out glowing embers: a romantic, relaxed night.

I ended up talking to Sue, as sometime during the evening Steve disappeared with one of Hugh's young Algerian friends. Not that I cared, as being with Sue was captivating. I loved listening to her talk about all the places she knew in Algeria.

Sue was attractive with a reddish glow to her face, probably from the fire, but her aura also glowed with excitement and a joy for living. I laughed at her stories of French and British workers she had known. Sitting next to her, with the fire hissing and popping and the wine flowing, I couldn't help but be drawn into a feeling, not of love, but of fascination and admiration.

Later that night, I drove them both home and told Sue I would sleep in the room next door. I showed her the bedroom and picked up a few things to take into the sitting room. Turning around, I was surprised to see she had slipped out of her dress and was standing enticingly in front of me.

"You've got a bed here; we can share it." She had a soft, come-on tone in her voice—beguiling and enticing.

Not having been with a woman for a few years, I felt nervous. She reached over, kissed me, and tickled the back of my neck. It electrified me, but I still wasn't sure.

"I have to leave in the morning—driving Steve down to Ghardaïa. He's an old friend."

"You told me. This is to thank you for letting me stay."

"We'll be gone—three or four days. You can . . ."

She kissed me again, reached down, and massaged me gently. I slipped down a slope, resistance failing me. Mixed emotions whirled around in my head. I was uneasy, drunk, and aroused.

"We shouldn't make too much noise. You know Steve is in the room next door and . . ." Sue touched my face and kissed me, softly and urgently.

"Shh," she said. "Stop thinking about him. This is for you."

I was conflicted. I knew it would upset him, but so what? We made love, and I tried not to make it obvious, but the sounds of sex are hard to conceal, and even though it must have been evident what we were doing, I gave up caring. The act of our passion together became the only thing of importance.

Afterwards, I fell asleep, but on waking horny in the early morning, I realized the bed was empty. *How had it been?* I found her in the kitchen, brewing coffee.

"Morning," I said a little hesitantly.

"Morning," she said and looked away.

"I woke up. You weren't there. I didn't know if . . ."

"You were tossing and turning so much. I got up to make some coffee."

"Oh. Umm, look, my flatmate might come back, but I'll give you a key. And you can . . ."

Had Susan regretted our night together? She still seemed friendly, but I was leaving for Ghardaïa with Steve. Bewildered, part of me wanted to stay, but I couldn't desert Steve.

◆ ◆ ◆

The drive down to Ghardaïa was five hours of either frigid silence or comments about how worthless I was.

"You fucked her, didn't you?"

"I slept with her, yes. She invited me into . . ."

"Her cunt, yes. I know about that."

"Don't be disgusting. What is it to you, anyway?"

"You don't know? This trip was supposed to be our reconciliation. You don't fucking care about me, do you?"

"Of course I do. It was—I couldn't . . ."

"Keep your dick in your pants. I know. What a prick you are! Why are we even doing this? Take me to the airport. I'll get a flight home."

Silence.

"Come on. One night? She probably won't even look at me again. She was thanking me for letting her stay in the flat. Forget it. Let's go on to Ghardaïa."

"You don't get it, do you? We're finished."

"It's no big deal."

"We are finished. I can't go on wanting you and then being ignored as you fuck the next guy or girl you meet."

"I don't. I haven't. I mean, That's the first time I've had sex with anyone else for . . ."

You're not gay, are you?"

"What?"

"Not 100%. You fucked her. You don't know what you are, do you?"

"What, so I would have been OK if I'd been with another guy? Hey, just a minute, I saw you with that Algerian guy. What happened there?"

"Nothing, we were just talking."

"Yeah, right. You left the party for a while, didn't you?"

"So?"

"Yeah, right. You can do whatever you like, and what? I'm supposed to be like you, but not with a woman? Is that it? That is so fucked up."

Silence.

"What about on the ferry from Marseilles, when you gave me a blow job?" *Why did I bring that up?*

"Yes, that's it. I gave you a blow job."

"Yeah, you did it as we pulled into port, and we were the last ones off the boat. The ferry hands were not well pleased." I laughed at the memory of them shaking their fists at us, thinking we had overslept.

We had an open relationship. He didn't live the life of a monk back in Manchester. I continued, probably digging myself into a deeper hole. "You know, we were getting on really well together. I enjoy being with you." Part of me knew I was lying or not telling the whole truth. He was challenging to be with, and this outburst served as another example of his erratic and jealous behavior.

More silence as I tried to think of something to say. The straight, monotonous road stretched into the distance. A gravel plain dotted with small dunes stretched out drearily on either side of us, and a light wind wafted plumes of fine sand grains from the dune crests. Sand settled on the highway and formed low drifts that I had to wind around.

The sun was high and bright, and its intensity added to a feeling of exhaustion. My mind kept wandering, and Steve's unbearable menace and silence didn't help. My eyes were closing, and my head was getting heavier. Then, veering around a bend, going too fast, I saw a truck speeding toward us: flashing lights and a horn blasting. I swerved to avoid the impending doom and just managed to keep the car upright as we hit the edge of the road. The truck thundered on. I stopped—shattered—and jumped out. Steve fumbled with his seat belt, struggled out of the car, and fell to the ground.

"You nearly killed me!" he screamed, pumped up by the intense shock of the near-death experience. "You stupid fucking arsehole," he yelled as he pulled himself up by hanging on to the open car door.

We were both high on the adrenalin rush that had flooded into our veins. "Shut the fuck up." I couldn't take his red-hot anger and walked away up the road.

"You're a selfish, self-centred bastard," he shouted at my back.

I turned and shouted back. "You've called me an arsehole. Now I'm a bastard as well. Fuck you."

I looked at the endless, monotonous, bleak landscape. Steve walked toward me, waving his arms and mumbling something I couldn't hear. I needed to pacify him but couldn't think of anything sensible to say.

"It's over. I have to give myself some dignity and not be treated like shit. Why did I waste years of my life over such a worthless jerk like you?"

I yelled back, "Well, you didn't waste years of your life, did you? What is this? Some theatrical piece you've been rehearsing? Were you some kind of celibate monk back in Manchester?"

I remembered some of the disreputable characters he had hooked up with for one-night stands, even here in Algeria. His duplicity and aggression disturbed me.

Mentally and physically exhausted and hyped up with adrenalin from the near-accident and his hostility, I sat on the roadside, taking deep breaths to calm myself and looking at the road receding to the distant horizon.

Eventually, the bleakness brought me back to the present reality. "If you want to fly back, OK. But we can't stay here, so let's drive on to Ghardaïa and check on flights. But it's a shame not to see the wonderful architectural gem of this city."

I sounded like a jerk. The hatred in Steve's eyes and the way he pulled at his long, straggly beard made me fear another outburst. Better not to speak. I started to count in my head, *One, two*—

"You really are an arrogant prick. I'm getting a flight from Ghardaïa. You can fuck off."

He was finishing it. I would be free of his incessant jealousy. His temper and aggressive behaviour had worn me down. We drove the two hundred kilometres to the airport in silence. Finally, with a sense of relief, I watched him leave.

Back in Bou Saada, Sue was still in my flat, so I volunteered to show her around. However, the town didn't seem quite normal. I detected a degree of tension in people. There were soldiers on the streets and in convoys on the roads. Driving home one day, a convoy of tank transporters and military trucks headed towards us, and a motorcycle cop waved us to the side of the road. We watched as the military convoy rumbled past.

That night, December 27th, the BBC World Service, announced that President Houari Boumédiène had died. It was covered the next day in the newspapers and on the TV. The country was shut down for days of mourning.

♦ ♦ ♦

Ten days later, a letter came from a theatre friend with an article from the *Manchester Evening News*. It stated that Steven Baddery, stage manager at Manchester Palace Theatre, had been found dead December the 26th. The report had the usual, *"The police are continuing their inquiries, and anyone with any information is urged . . ."*

His friend wrote that Steve had been attacked late at night while walking back from a gay activist meeting. He had spoken quite openly about police brutality against young gay men. His body was dragged out of the canal in the early hours of the following day. The autopsy report stated he had been badly beaten then thrown into the canal, where he drowned. I couldn't read anymore.

Later, I looked at some of the photographs we'd taken on our trip through France. It was painful looking at them. Another chapter in my life had closed, but it ended when I saw him leave on the flight to Algiers. We hadn't even said goodbye.

I cried for a lost friend, as the brutality of the attack quite sickened me. How much had our break-up affected Steve? It hadn't been pleasant, and his anger at me may have also been a bigger fury against the treatment of gay people in general.

However, I mourned the loss of someone I could joke around with and talk about things I could never say to anyone else.

However, being owned by Steve was too exhausting and claustrophobic. He had wanted me for himself yet still demanded the freedom to have sex with anyone he fancied. I couldn't go back for the funeral: it would have been hypocritical. I had to move on and not be tied down by the past. I'd never played an active part in the gay scene being a wallflower rather than a participant. In Algeria, the emptiness and beauty of the desert freed me and the friendship with Moussa and Sue had created a new world of love and mutual respect. I felt alive, and it was like being reborn.

ELEVEN

Today, sitting at my favorite café, the tempting aroma of roasting juicy chickens turning on the spit outside was overwhelming. It was market day, and I watched the life of Bou Saâda strolling past. Bearded older men chatted and bargained with the vegetable sellers. A few youths in loose shirts and their best tight white jeans strutted past the young women chaperoned by their mothers. A mating game—to see and be seen.

"Hey, Dave, how are you?" A friendly voice. I turned and saw the smiling face of my friend.

"Moussa. I'm good. How are you?"

"Fine. I have not seen you for a long time." I motioned to the empty seat and called for the waiter. *"Asma khawadja!"* It translated directly as, "Listen, coffee-server!"

Moussa sat down, looking genuinely pleased to see me. Then looking straight at me, his eyes twinkling with the natural ability to engulf the person he was talking to, he asked. "Where have you been?"

"I bought a car in the UK and drove down to Ghardaïa with a friend."

"You have car?" He winked at me, and I dreaded his next question. "So, you are free. Come to the hammam and then we have dinner tonight?"

"Yes. That would be nice. We can catch up on all the news." I was relieved he didn't start talking about all the girls we could pick up. I loved spending time with him, relaxing and catching up on all the stories of life in the town.

"Come, let's go."

We spent an hour sweating, being scrubbed, and then relaxing under the towels: an enervating experience. Afterward, lying under the towels and recovering, you felt clean and fresh, convinced the world had become a better place.

Moussa invited me back to his house for the evening meal. We sat in the *majlis* in his home, the area reserved for guests and male family members. His mother had prepared a typical Algerian meal—couscous with a delicious spicy sauce and chicken, chickpeas, and carrots. A large serving bowl heaped with couscous sat in the centre of the room with bowls of the sauce arranged around it. Sitting cross-legged on the floor, we ate. After we'd finished, Moussa's younger brother entered and cleared away the plates. Moussa had already explained the rest of the family ate after us. It made me feel guilty, but that was the custom.

Moussa took me to his room and put on some of his records. I recognized the singer. "The Egyptian woman? I forget, what's her name?"

"Umm Kalthoum. Listen. She has beauty in her voice. She sings of love and loss. Her voice rises and falls. It is so beautiful. How do you say? Mes . . . mesma?"

"Mesmerizing?"

"Yes. Poetic. Romantic."

Her voice, accompanied by violins, haunted the room, and together they created powerful, slow, emotive moments. Then the music rose to high-pitched eerie tones, sending shivers down my spine.

Moussa stood and slowly gyrated his upper body, his hands above his head, twisting and turning in time with the music. He beckoned me to dance with him, so I rose and closed my eyes, flowing around the room with the notes of her ethereal ballad. Our languorous bodies touched and blended into one drifting spirit. Moussa, his hot breath on my neck, whispered, "I love how you dance. I am so glad we are friends."

"Me too. You are such a wonderful dancer. You float around the room so beautifully."

He stroked my cheek and kissed my neck. Undulating as one with the music, we turned to face each other. Moussa was charming, and close up, his musky aroma—earthy and woody—smelled erotic and sensual. I felt safe and protected in his arms, and I knew I would explore his body and feel the strength and warmth of his tenderness.

◆ ◆ ◆

The next day, he came to the flat while Elizabeth and I chatted, enjoying a glass of wine. When I introduced them, I saw the sparkle in his eyes, and Moussa, ever the charmer, greeted her, bowed, and kissed her hand. Elizabeth giggled a little and blushed.

He was wearing tight blue jeans and a dark blue T-shirt, showing his muscular biceps. I'd undressed him last night and remembered the silky smoothness of his skin, but now he was preening himself in front of Liz. It was almost as if he'd known she'd be here. I smiled because I knew exactly the kind of impression, he would make on her. He was incredibly sexy with the typical Arab short curly hair, a shadow of a beard, and a trimmed mustache. Today he oozed sex appeal, but not just that, he was more sophisticated than many Algerians, and his English had improved remarkably in these last few months.

Moussa smiled and sat next to her. There weren't many places to sit, but it seemed a little forward. Elizabeth was wearing her usual Indian print dress and a white blouse, without a bra: quite revealing, which must have been evident to Moussa.

We chatted, or, to tell the truth, Elizabeth chatted with Moussa, gushing on about Algeria. "I do love Algeria. It is so fascinating. I've been here a few months now, but don't know any Algerians."

"I am glad you like it. Let me be your guide."

Oh, oh, I thought, *here's Moussa doing his suave side.* I could see him shifting his body around to face her and projecting his gorgeous infectious smile straight at her. Turning on the charm, I could see it oozing out of every pore. *No, I'm not jealous. He's a charmer and a philanderer.* He was open about it, and I knew too well what jealousy could do to a friendship.

"Hey, I'm hungry," I said, "Why not go out to the Transat or the Caïd and get something to eat?"

Moussa immediately jumped in. "Come to my house. We can have dinner and talk freely."

"I'd love to go," Elizabeth said, looking pleadingly at me.

"Yes, that's very kind of you. If you think your parents wouldn't mind, Moussa?"

"No. You are my guests. Come."

"Thank you. You are very generous."

The fact that Elizabeth would get to see inside an Arab's house made me feel happy, and I hadn't failed to notice how sparkling she had become.

"Oh, it is nothing. This is our custom. Come, let's go."

"Thank you," said Elizabeth. "Give me a minute. I will go and change."

◆ ◆ ◆

That was the start of an intense friendship. I noticed he didn't talk about all the girls he knew. He went on about how beautiful Elizabeth was and how he felt about her. *Is it because she's English? Getting a passport out of Algeria?* One time, when we were alone, I asked him how he felt about Elizabeth.

"I love her, Dave, but I can't tell her because I'm afraid she will think I just want her for passport. Oh, yes, many Algerians try for passport. But not me. I can't stop thinking of her, but I can't say . . ." He paused and looked helpless.

We sat facing each other on low foam mattresses scattered on the floor. I'd made a pot of tea and put a few biscuits on a plate in the centre of the room, but Moussa wasn't interested.

"Tell her. I know she likes you. She is attracted to you. You can see it in her eyes. I'm sure she loves you too. You are exotic, striking even, with those beautiful brown eyes."

"Exotic? What do you mean? I am curious thing to her?" This made him sit up and look at me with a hurt look in his eyes. "I am someone she can play with and then leave when she returns to England?"

"No, I didn't mean . . . I meant you are attractive, cool, exciting, but . . ."

"Oh yes, always but. But what, Dave?"

"Don't get too attached. How many girls have you had and then left? I don't want you to hurt her by dumping her when you get bored with her."

"What? How you can say this?" He looked bewildered that I could even think he would find anyone else. "You don't understand. I love Elizabeth. She is so much different from others. I cannot even compare. I have never felt like this before."

Talking to him was like talking to a love-sick teenager. He even told me they hadn't had sex yet, which surprised me.

TWELVE

That weekend of January 19, Seamus had taken Thursday off sick but went with some of his French friends to Algiers. Upon his return, the police arrested him, and we never saw him again. Some French teachers had also been arrested but were released. *Because of the special relationship between France and Algeria? No, that's conjecture.* But even so, we were all stunned. What had happened? Surely not because he had been absent for a day?

Strike Five.

♦ ♦ ♦

Susan was friends with *la surveillante générale* at the girls' school, who told Susan what had happened two weeks after Seamus had left. Algeria, being a police state, had informants everywhere. She warned Sue that someone was watching us even if we didn't know it. However, like in East Germany, you never knew who would report you. One of these informants must have been at the drinking session the night of Beau's party. It made you think about who you could trust, but all the Algerians I had met and my high-school students seemed friendly and open. I knew I could spend time with my Algerian friends but not cross certain lines, such as politics and religion. Seamus had crossed those lines on more than one occasion. He felt he was immune, but he had come to the local police's attention, and they compiled a report concerning his anti-Algerian activities. The *surveillante générale* swore Sue to secrecy and then showed her the cover letter sent to the school. "I never liked him," she said dismissively.

Mr. Seamus Breedon:
1. *Dressed inappropriately, walking about town in see-through clothing.*
2. *Gave pornographic material to corrupt an Algerian youth.*
3. *Taught sex in school to 15-year-old Algerian girls.*
4. *Met with young Algerian men, persuaded them to drink alcohol, insulted the President, and made remarks against Algeria's legitimate government.*
5. *Engaged in political activity.*

In conclusion, his total disregard for the norms and disrespect for Algeria's customs and culture makes him unfit to be a teacher. Therefore, the recommendation is to expel him immediately.

◆ ◆ ◆

Now we had some context and could see how all those little things added up. I knew he had been friendly with some of the French and Algerian teachers, and it seemed that Seamus, as a foreigner, had stepped over the line. Then I remembered the night of the party a few weeks ago when he had disappeared quietly, and Jean Jacques, a physics teacher at my school, had been with him. Hadn't he gone to Algiers with Jean Jacques and a couple of the other French teachers?

His arrest and disappearance provided the week's gossip for the town, but we didn't really know anything. However, it spread a feeling of fear among the expats that they could be removed for what seemed like arbitrary reasons.

♦ ♦ ♦

On February 9, we read in *Le Monde* that Chadli Benjedid had been appointed President. Another FLN man, but one more moderate and with a desire to introduce reforms.

To tell the truth, I wasn't really following internal politics. We continued teaching, and Liz kept talking about how she would enact revenge on Beau, but it was moving slowly.

THIRTEEN

I didn't see Moussa until he returned for the summer holiday. School had finished, and it was a tense time for us, but we had to wait for June's paycheck to make the final transfer before leaving.

One evening, I noticed a light in Elizabeth's front room, so I knocked on her door, and she opened it, dragging me inside and closing it behind her.

"Hi," I said, "I haven't seen you for a while, so I thought I'd drop by and see how you were doing."

"Moussa is here."

"Moussa, good to see you."

"You too, Dave. We were coming to see you. We need you for assistance."

"With what?" I asked innocently.

Liz interrupted, "We're working on a way to deal with Beau. We need you to drive your car."

"Yeah, but we can't use my car. It is, as the French say, '*En panne*'—buggered. It'll be a few days before I can get it back."

"That's OK. Moussa can borrow one."

I must say I felt nervous as the stakes were high. "But it could be dangerous."

"I don't care. I want satisfaction. Will you help?"

"Yes, I told you. But what exactly can we do?"

We talked about their plan to humiliate him and tried to make it feasible. Still, nothing mattered to Elizabeth as she wanted her "pound of flesh." We discussed it well into the night and eventually came up with a final plan.

◆ ◆ ◆

Daytime temperatures reached about thirty-five degrees. The heat sucked the moisture out of your body, and a strong, steady wind blew red sand from the Sahara. The fine grit sandblasted cars and any exposed skin felt gritty. We stayed in during the day and went out at night when the hot, dry wind had died down, but you still felt uncomfortable even in shorts and a T-shirt.

The night of retribution was hot and stuffy. We sat in Moussa's friend's beat-up Renault 4, watching Beau's place and waiting for the signal. We had agreed Moussa would give us two flashes of light, a pause, and then a further one. After the sign, Liz had to go through the open back door and into the kitchen, then enter the sitting room to take photos of Beau. My role was a mere getaway driver.

We waited, and by midnight, we'd been there for what seemed like hours. The boredom and heat were intolerable. Then the signal; the torchlight flashed from inside the kitchen at the back. Liz put on a headscarf to cover her face and hair, grabbed her camera, and quickly made her way across to the house, entering by the back door. A few minutes later, she ran out, followed by Moussa. They jumped in the car; I turned the key and roared off with the tires throwing up clouds of choking dust.

Moussa, laughing, said, "It is OK. I hide his car keys. We do it!" Triumphant, he laughed again.

"Wait till we get those photos developed. We've got Beau."

Moussa had seduced Beau. They had "accidentally" met in town, where Moussa had pretended to be distressed because he had missed the last bus to Algiers. Beau invited him back to his place to eat, and events took their course.

A friend of Moussa's had a photo-shop, a hole-in-the-wall operation, and he developed the photos. I was a little concerned, but Moussa assured me his friend would do anything for fifty American dollars. We eagerly pounced on them to see what they showed. Beau, naked in the first photo, is lying on the mattress with a man next to him. You couldn't see the man's face, but the position left nothing to the imagination. In the second, Beau's face is visible, looking straight at the camera, utterly shocked.

Two days later, we took the photos over to Beau's. I came too because I didn't want to miss out on his humiliation.

Liz did the talking. "I want a thousand dollars US, and you get a posting somewhere else next year. You'll get the negatives and these photographs. If not, the photos will be handed over to the police. Moussa has friends. They'll be released to the newspapers. You can say goodbye to your job here."

Beau was overwhelmed. "But why did you do this? Why?"

"You don't know?" Liz shouted at him. "You don't know? Because of the bet."

"*Mon Dieu.* I didn't do it for a bet."

"Rubbish. You had a bet you could seduce me, and you won, what two thousand dinars?"

Beau caved immediately. "I'm sorry. I didn't . . ." Shock and defeat clearly showed on his face.

"I don't care," Liz shouted, implacable in her desire for reprisal. "A thousand dollars US or we release the photos. We will come back in three days."

We stood and left. I felt sorry for Beau. He looked so defeated, but I had to show solidarity with Liz and Moussa.

FOURTEEN

The heat was intense, and the desire to have a fresh, cooling breeze was overwhelming, but it wasn't just the heat. A stink of decay permeated itself into our consciousness: sickening and affecting our moods, making us irritable and cranky.

We left in the early evening as the town woke from its afternoon slumber. Nearing the bottom of the hill, we gagged at the nauseating sweet, sickly smell of death. We spotted the corpse of a donkey lying grotesquely in a ditch with a million flies buzzing on and around it.

As we drove on, I said ominously, "Some people would think that's an omen. A premonition."

"Shut up!" Liz said. "It's just a donkey hit by a car at night."

"I've never seen anything like that in all my time in Algeria."

"It happens," Moussa commented, trying to sound as matter-of-fact as he could.

"Forget it!" shouted Liz. "We are getting revenge. No omens."

We found Beau in a state of total despair. "I'm so sorry you think I would do this. You know who? Jean Jacques . . . he's evil . . . Seamus' friend. I knew him from before. He made me—"

Elizabeth interrupted him. "What are you talking about? What do you mean you knew him from before?"

"Explain." Moussa said and looked at Beau as he spoke. It wasn't a look I'd seen before.

"I knew him in France." Beau moaned. "We went to the same university for a year. In Paris. I was doing my teacher training and he was studying politics."

"Stop." Moussa turned to look at Elizabeth and said, "Dave, take Liz back. I'll come and see you later."

"What?" Elizabeth demanded.

He looked at me. "Dave, take her home. Do not talk anything to anyone. Understand?"

I could see Moussa wasn't joking. The charm had gone. I felt afraid, remembering how Seamus had disappeared. Simulating a friendlier tone, I said, "OK, I'll take her to Sue's apartment. It may not smell as bad. Later, tell us what's going on."

I tried not to look anxious and took Elizabeth by the arm to walk her out the door. At first, she resisted, pulling away from me, but one look at Moussa's face persuaded her to walk out with me.

Sue lived in a different part of town where the smell of death wasn't as noticeable. Even so, we lit candles. I asked Sue to comfort Liz as she was upset and unsure about what had ensued. Shocked by this sudden change of events, we felt afraid that we, too, would be deported. Neither Elizabeth nor I could get over the change that had happened when he had ordered us to leave. How could he have been so charming and friendly? How much was a lie?

A sense of doubt, like a shadow, crept silently into the room as we sat, waiting and fearing the worst. Arrest? Deportation?

Liz had admitted earlier that her plot for revenge had not given her the satisfaction she had expected. She started to reiterate what she had already said. "What's the point? Moussa is not the man I knew. I can't stay. My sense of security has been ripped away."

"It's OK." Sue comforted her and tried to remain calm despite the catch in her throat. "Let's wait to see what Moussa has to say. He wanted to talk to Beau alone."

"They did it to Seamus. Do you think we are any different? We're not free here. Moussa is Algerian. He can do what he likes, and did you see how he changed?"

I tried to sound nonchalant and carefree, but it belied my anxiety and nagging doubts of uncertainty. "There's nothing we can do. I love it here. I want to stay, but if we have to go, then so what? It's just the way it is."

Liz wouldn't let it drop. She kept on asking questions and commenting. "Jean Jacques? Dave, you know him? He does have a look of evil about him. Those intense black eyes."

"Oh, come on. Jean Jacques is just a teacher here like the rest of us. Let's wait for Moussa. Despite it all, I have confidence in him."

They both gave snorts of derision at my attempt to give him the benefit of the doubt. I couldn't believe that he had changed so much, but my friends were afraid and wondered about how abruptly their naivety and concept of safety had been destroyed.

Moussa knocked on the door. The knocking seemed so loud and threatening that I jumped, thinking the police had come to arrest us. It's incredible what tricks the imagination can play with your mind. My heart pounding, I cracked open the door and peered into the corridor. Moussa stood there alone and smiled confidently.

I stood back to allow him to enter. He walked into the room and looked around, seeing Elizabeth and Susan looking up at him with thinly disguised fear. "What's the matter with you all? I want to talk to Beau and find out what he know."

He continued smiling and sat on one of the mats, facing us. "Do not worry. This is not touching you. You have nothing to worry. Jean Jacques is doing this to attack him about Paris, years ago."

We were all bursting with questions, but the loudest came from Elizabeth. "What?"

"I can't say. It is not important."

She shouted in utter frustration, "Are you police?"

"No, I am medical student. You know this." He sounded genuine, his voice quiet and calming to reassure us. This was the Moussa we knew—or thought we had known.

"No, we do not," Liz stated quite bluntly. She felt hurt and now distrusted the man with whom she had become infatuated. "We know nothing about you. You were a different man there. You acted like you were police in charge of some undercover operation."

Silence. We waited for Moussa to speak, wondering how much he would say and reveal. He looked at us and grimaced in a slightly boyish way. He was still roguishly attractive, and I couldn't stop liking him and desiring his soft caresses. Feeling a little overwhelmed, I shook my head to clear it.

"OK. You must all swear secrecy. You cannot talk what I tell. If you do, I cannot help. Understand?"

We all agreed, relieved we'd get to know what was going on. Moussa's tone was calm, and I wanted to believe him, despite all that had happened in the last few hours.

"I am not secret police. When we become friends, I am not watching you." Moussa said, looking at Elizabeth.

"Can we believe you? I don't know if I can." Elizabeth still sounded hurt and angry.

I knew how she felt but wanted to listen to him.

"Let I—me speak." *He must be getting tired,* I thought, *or stressed.* Liz gave the man she cared for a long, penetrating look.

"No, do not judge. Let me finish, please."

She nodded reluctantly.

"You know, when we want revenge for Seamus, I talk to people. I know important people. One of my friends at university. His father is Interior Ministry."

"They run the interior police, don't they? What are they called? The *Sûreté?*" I asked.

Moussa looked at me and snorted, "Yes. I explain the situation of Seamus, then Beau, and what we want to do. Seamus is friend with Jean Jacques, but I did not know *Sûreté* watching him."

My head was swimming. "So Seamus . . . is a spy?" *What a bizarre word. In books and films? Yes. But Seamus?*

"No. But he is involved. Seamus easy. They have no problem deporting him, but they need know if Beau work with French. It go back to Algerian Revolution. He is Breton and born, here, in Algeria."

This is incredible. Too much to process and too many questions. "What about you? You were, what, recruited?" I asked. "What about us? Are we being watched as well?"

"Oh, come on. This is French–Algerian thing. The *Sûreté*—no argument with British."

"Yeah, but it seems they didn't mind getting rid of the Irish." Now I wasn't sure what I could believe.

"He meet with French and talk politics. Remember when Seamus go to Algiers? Not for holiday."

"What? What did Seamus do?"

"Oh," Moussa continued brusquely, "he carry papers from French embassy. More? I don't know."

"How does this connect to Beau?"

"The police want? No—wanted a reason to make Beau talk. Seduction they think good idea."

"Did they know he liked men?"

"Yes. They know."

"What will happen to him?"

"It depend what he know and tell them. He will not come back to Bou Saâda, but maybe he can help."

I couldn't ask in front of Susan. What do they know about Moussa and me? Then, do they know about Elizabeth? God, this is getting too complicated.

"What about you?" asked Elizabeth.

"I am finished. Now, I will continue my study."

"Can you still come to England as we had planned?" Liz asked.

"Yes. I have passport."

Susan interrupted, "What about Jean Jacques? He hasn't been arrested, has he?"

Moussa continued, "No. Some questions you should not ask. The police interview you tomorrow. Don't worry. I will be there."

It was 2 a.m. Exhausted, I motioned to Susan and we got up. "You can both sleep on the mattresses in here." I nodded at Moussa and Elizabeth. "Goodnight."

Once in bed, I fell asleep almost straight away, but Susan was tossing and turning and woke me with questions about what had happened. We became aware of noises coming from the sitting room, so we both strained our ears and realized we could hear Liz panting and moaning and Moussa's soft grunting. Their love-making went on for quite a while. Then Moussa reached orgasm, letting out a muffled shout, and Liz giggled, followed by, "Shh. They can hear us."

Inspired and horny, we followed with our version. It was a little quicker, but I'm sure just as passionate, though I didn't shout and Susan didn't giggle.

FIFTEEN

In the morning, I met Alain, one of the older and more serious French teachers, at the corner shop. I took the opportunity to ask him about the Algerian secret police and told him I was worried about Seamus. He responded in French in an arrogant, disdainful way only the French can manage. He basically told me that the *Sûreté* is controlled by the Ministry of the Interior, like MI5 fighting against terrorism, espionage, or coups intent on overthrowing the government. That certainly didn't put my mind at rest.

Liz, Sue, and I were questioned separately at the Transat Hotel. It was an old French colonial hotel with a lot of faded charm, but Moussa told us this made it less conspicuous. He led me to a private room, introduced me to Captain Touati, and left.

The captain told me to sit down, and he sat in the other armchair. He was polite, charming, and pleasant, and it was all relaxed with a few basic questions about my background. He asked me about Jean Jacques.

"I hardly know him. He teaches maths and physics at my school, but we don't have much to say. He keeps himself aloof— apart from people."

"Did you see him with Seamus?"

"Well, yes," I said. "I saw them together a few times, but I didn't take much notice. Seamus spoke better French than me and I thought they were friends."

"How did you meet Moussa?"

I shifted uncomfortably in my chair, speculating about what Moussa might have said. "We met on the bus when I first arrived in Bou Saâda. He showed me around, and we sometimes meet when he's back from university. He's a friend."

I didn't go into details, and the captain didn't ask any further questions about Moussa.

"When will you be leaving?"

"When we get June's salary and can make the transfer."

"Are you coming back for a second year?"

I countered with a question I had wanted to ask. "I don't know. Will it be OK to return next year?"

"Yes, if you want to. We have reports from your *proviseur*, who is happy with the way you teach, and your contract has been renewed. I have a copy here." He tapped his briefcase. "Do you intend to return?"

"I'd like to. I enjoy working here and travelling around looking at the country. It's beautiful."

I wanted to give a good impression so he'd think we wanted to return. It was the only job I had, but it wasn't only about the money, as Sue and I both enjoyed living and working in Algeria.

"Thank you, David. Give a contact address to the sergeant where we can reach you if we need to. You will get your contract soon. Here. My card."

I thanked him, and he got up to walk me to the door. We shook hands as I left. I felt relieved. It hadn't been unpleasant, rather the opposite—friendly and informal.

Outside, Moussa said, "OK?" I nodded. "Let's meet tomorrow for plan. Meet me *Café des Sports* six in afternoon."

◆ ◆ ◆

In Bou Saâda, we prepared to leave in what we hoped would be a few days. It was still hot outside, but the evenings were cooler.

I told Susan I had to see Moussa, and she told me to be careful. She went back to her place to pack and get ready for our holiday, though we hadn't booked any flights yet.

I drove to the centre of town. The dead donkey had been taken away. I wound down the window to get some semblance of cool air circulating. The familiar smells of Bou Saâda returned: the dryness of sand, the aroma of wood fires for cooking, a whiff of perfume from a jasmine bush, and the sweetness of oranges being cut up in the juice bar. Nine months ago, I would have walked, and thinking about it now, I wasn't sure why I drove. Parking was always tricky, yet I somehow felt safer with the car's metal around me. I kept looking in the rear-view mirror to see if anyone was following me.

Dread, fear, and apprehension fomented in my stomach, along with a realization that we were in a situation larger than anyone had imagined. One day I felt fine, but at other times the doubts returned. *Paranoia?* I wondered whether we should come back next year.

The café in the newer part of town was popular with the younger generation of Algerian men. I knew there wouldn't be any women there. It was an entirely male occupation to sit in cafés and talk loudly about football and rivalries between teams. I sat at a table on the other side of the street to observe people walking past. *I'm thinking like a spy. How strange.*

It wasn't too busy, but pleasant enough in the heart of town, with a comforting feeling that I belonged. Looking around, I noticed a truck arrive and stop. The driver clambered out, leaving his engine running. The blue smoke and diesel fumes spread across the road, making my eyes water and cough. *Why doesn't someone tell him to turn it off?*

A few young men sitting at one of the tables opposite were talking and laughing. Then one of them turned and shouted at the driver. A few choice words in Arabic, and he ran back to switch his truck off. I realized those young men weren't just boys off the street out enjoying the cooler evening air. Then I saw Farid, a student who had recently completed school, sitting with them. He waved at me. I watched him approach, knowing I had to be polite. *Why had Moussa chosen such a public place to meet? How do I get rid of him?*

"Farid. *Bonsoir. Ça va?* Good to see you."

He was an excellent student from a prominent family. His father owned the largest chemist shop in Bou Saâda and was chairman of the District Council, called the *Wilaya*. Farid had talked about their visits to England, Germany, and France. Being wealthy, they had a paddock outside town with horses, a swimming pool, and a weekend house. He had invited me to visit, but I declined, not wanting to be accused of bias in marking his papers.

Algeria is a socialist country, but one where the authoritative members of the FLN (*Front de Libération Nationale*) could obtain items of prestige well beyond the imagination of the ordinary man in the street. The FLN had been at the forefront of the war against the French. After the Algerian Revolution, they had installed themselves in the government, controlling every level of power. It was a one-party state professing socialist principles but wasn't so good about spreading the wealth around.

Farid had been a pleasant, well-mannered student with a confident air, but I had to remind myself that Farid's father had influence in the town, so I had to be polite and show how pleased I was to see him. Even so, I just wanted him gone.

"Mister David. How are you?"

"Good evening, Farid. I'm fine. But please, call me Dave. You're not a student anymore."

Farid was eighteen, short, with intense brown eyes and straight, black hair brushed back away from his forehead. I'd always seen him as well-mannered, but serious and more mature than the other students. Now, standing in front of me, he smiled in a relaxed and friendly manner.

"How are your plans for university?"

"I'm waiting for results of the Bac. exam."

"I'm sure you will do well. You're a good student."

I hoped the conversation would end with the basic greetings, and then he'd leave.

"Moussa asked me to come find you."

"What?" I said, surprised. *What is going on now?* "Do you know Moussa well?"

"We are cousins."

"Of course, you're all cousins here, aren't you?" I laughed a little nervously.

He ignored my comment. "Can I join you?"

My warning-danger alarm bell was ringing. I had to be polite but . . . I nodded. Farid sat down and asked the waiter for tea, calling out, "*Khawadja zoodge chai.*"

"So, Moussa wanted you to find me? What did he say?"

"He is busy and said not to worry. He tell me to help you."

"Oh," I said, a little shocked. And then I asked in a calmer voice, "What did he tell you?"

"About Beau. I know." He spoke in a casual, almost disinterested way.

"Oh God." I groaned and then immediately said, "Sorry, I didn't mean to offend you."

"That's OK, Mister David. Dave, sorry." He laughed self-consciously. "I have been to England, you know." *Now he sounds self-important. What's going on?*

The waiter arrived and put two glasses of tea on the table in front of us. Before I could react, Farid paid him. I offered him money, but Farid brushed my hand away. With the waiter gone, I continued, "Why did Moussa send you and not tell me this himself?"

"He is busy. Moussa says it is good you stay and let your friends leave tomorrow night."

"What?" I asked again, shocked he knew so much about us. He had been my student only a few weeks ago. "Why does Moussa think they should leave early?"

"Dave, talk with Moussa. I will take you there."

I needed time to think. The tea was hot and sweet, and I blew on it to cool it before taking a few sips. When I had first arrived, I asked for tea with no sugar, not understanding they brewed it in one pot and added sugar before serving. Now I needed the shock of sweetness to give me the energy to continue with this charade. Drinking it, sip after sip, I realized I knew very little of what was actually going on.

Putting the tea glass down, I opened by moving my bishop into a good strategic position. "Look, I'm sorry, Farid. I like you. You are a good student, but I can't change my plans because Moussa says to. I'm leaving. We're all flying out together." My voice rose a little. Fed up with all these games, I wanted out.

Farid listened, smiled, but didn't speak. He sipped from his tea glass. This was like playing chess, both of us plotting our moves. Farid was a good-looking guy but a little short for most Algerians. However, I detected an element of cunning in his features. "Come, I will take you to see Moussa." I hadn't seen his knight take my queen. "We go in your car to Al Caïd. Moussa is there."

"How did you know I came in my car?"

"I saw you arrive in it."

"You mean, you've been watching me and . . ."

"I wanted to see if anyone following. I wait and watch."

"Fuck. I'm sorry, Farid, but I'm getting fed up with this." I knew the game was almost over.

The men at the other table laughed loudly and looked around at us. One looked directly at Farid and twisted his wrist with his fingers raised in a gesture meaning, *What's up?* Farid shook his head.

"Mister David, I've never heard you say bad words before."

I shrugged. I didn't care anymore. The men got up, and as they passed, they said something in Arabic to Farid. He replied by shaking his head.

"What did they say?"

"Nothing. About the football game tonight."

I don't know what to believe. I was weak and vulnerable. I moved a pawn forward two squares. "Look, I'm not afraid to tell you, but I've had enough. I'm not going to see your cousin. We're leaving on the first plane out of here."

Farid didn't react. His move now. Leaning toward me, he spoke in a soft, confidential voice, "Dave, now is difficult to get flights out of Algiers. The holidays. Help us, we can get any day you want."

A threat? True, getting flights at the beginning of the school holidays would be difficult. We couldn't leave until the school gave permission for our exit visas, and I needed to make the June salary transfer. *'We can get you any day you want?' We?* He'd made his move, and I had to concede.

♦ ♦ ♦

Half an hour later, Moussa, Farid, and I were sitting in an air-conditioned room in the Caïd Hotel. The Pouillon-designed hotel was impressive and fortress-like, making it the most appropriate place to meet with the secret police. Moussa ordered bottles of beer for the two of us and Fanta for Farid. We sat and talked, but despite the friendliness, I felt suspicious and was on my guard. *Had I been set up for something?*

Moussa looked directly at me, smiled, and said in a pleasant, calm voice, "We need you to do what Algerians cannot."

"Look. I'm sorry. I like working here, but I'm flying home and then to the States in a few days. This has all been too much. I'm thinking of not returning after the holidays." *There, I'd said it. Not a wise thing to say, but I want it out in the open.*

Moussa ignored me. "Maybe it is better for Susan and Elizabeth to leave first. They will not . . ." Moussa hesitated, searching for a word to pacify me with. "They will not worry for you. They can stay at hotel in London. They will shop and you can stay for a few days."

The crashing in my head made me want to jump up and run. *Fight or flight? They won't worry about me?* "I've told you I'm leaving." I stood up and walked over to the window. A few swaying palm trees and blue sky. I watched birds circling over distant acacia trees. *Crows? Doves? No. Pigeons, you idiot. Am I trapped in this game they are playing? I'd had so much fun with Moussa. Now?*

"Dave. Sit down. We need you help us. Then you can leave," Moussa spoke quietly and smoothly.

"A threat? I can't believe it."

"Please do not be so, so, what's the word, melo-? . . . Melo-?"

"Melodramatic? You think I'm being melodramatic?" Now I was shouting while pacing the room, having ignored his request to sit down.

"Sorry. I playing with words. Look, I know I can trust you to help we . . . us."

"Are you buttering me up?"

"What is buttering up?"

"Flattering me, making me feel good, so I will do whatever you want?"

"Buttering up. I will remember." I could see Moussa filing it away for some future use, his lips moving as he silently repeated the expression. *Buttering me up.* A light smile flittered around his face. *Buttering me up.* Rolling the words around and playing with them. "No, I'm not buttering you up." Moussa shook his head. He became like the friend I knew. "Dave, I am sorry. I desperate. Police have blackmailed me. Yes? We have to do this together. You got to help me or . . ."

"Or what?"

Moussa shrugged.

"What?"

"I do not know, Dave. I will tell you, but not now. I need you—help, please."

Tears formed, and his look of vulnerability and fear rekindled my feelings for him despite everything. *What can I do? Is he being melodramatic? What options do I have?* Feeling numb, I sat—thinking or not—just sitting. He looked so desperate and his pleading . . . Eventually, I nodded, accepting the inevitable. "OK. What do you want me to do?"

Moussa exhaled. "Thank you, Dave. We will do this together. Farid can get Liz and Sue tickets for tomorrow." I remembered Farid was in the room, and he'd said nothing. *Has he seen how easily I can be manipulated?*

◆ ◆ ◆

That night, I explained to Sue what had happened and how we had no other option. It was hot and stuffy in the room. The din of car horns and throaty, roaring motorbikes added to a fog of unpleasantness hanging over us. We'd lost control of our lives and, like pieces of flotsam, were being tossed by an uncontrollable tide. I felt a degree of desperation in clinging to her knowing all we had was our love for each other. Nothing else mattered.

Sue, Liz, and I left early the next morning for the long drive to Algiers. We met Moussa at the Air Algerie check-in desk.

Moussa, like a proud cockerel, smiled at Liz. "I'm sorry, but Farid could only get you these." He handed the tickets to Liz.

She looked and exclaimed, "Business class?"

"Yes. Oh, vouchers for five nights in hotel, and money for shopping. Dave and I join you after three or four days. Do not worry. It all be OK."

Liz giggled, leaned forward and patted Moussa on his right cheek. "This is great. Thank you, Moussy."

He blushed and looked pleased and embarrassed at the same time.

We helped Sue and Liz check in, then waved goodbye as they went through to the Departure Lounge. Depressed to see them go but resigned, I walked out of the airport with Moussa. *We'd been bought. Now what do I have to do?*

SIXTEEN

Later in the afternoon, Captain Touati knocked on our hotel room door and strode in wearing a perfectly pressed khaki uniform, shiny black shoes, and a military cap. Moussa and I—in jeans and T-shirts—looked like beach bums in comparison. Touati pretended not to notice and took command of the meeting.

"Please sit down. This is just informal. Thank you, Dave, for coming. Let me go straight to the point. We need you to rendezvous with Jean Jacques."

He must have been on some American training course, I thought.

"Yes, engage with him. You were friendly with Seamus, and Jean Jacques knows this."

"Not exactly friendly, but yes." I looked at the glass of tea on the table but couldn't bring myself to pick it up. He would see my hands shaking.

Captain Touati didn't hesitate. "You must talk to him and make him meet you. You will tell him you have papers from Seamus for him."

He continued talking, outlining the plan. It sounded deceptively simple, and I persuaded myself I was getting us out of a difficult situation. *What were the papers about? Seamus had been very aggressive about the political situation in Algeria. Maybe*

he'd said too much, and a dissident group had contacted him?
The lure of double the salary. I caved. I had no other choice.

I was needed as someone who knew him and who could meet
Jean Jacques on neutral ground. The captain left us to work out
the details, but it had to be within the next few days. He mentioned we would be watched for our protection. He didn't tell
us why or what I had to communicate with Jean Jacques: "Need
to know," he had said. Obviously, I didn't need to know, but the
exact details? I shrugged, knowing I was a pawn in a game far
more extensive than I could envisage. Actually, it didn't matter . .
. just do the job and be finished with it.

After leaving the room, Moussa led me into the gardens, where
he said we couldn't be overheard. We sat on one of the benches
and let the sun warm us after the intense cold of the air conditioner.

"I must tell you why I so . . . so . . . involved. Yes. It is student
at university. Beautiful and she, how can I say? She . . . Now, I
understand, but then I did not know . . ." We were sitting side by
side—easy for him to look not at me, but at the mimosa trees in
front of us.

"What are you trying to say, you idiot?" I was enjoying his
obvious discomfort but wanted him to move the story along.

"We became friends, good friends. You know what I mean?"

"Your dick does get around, doesn't it?" Being sarcastic, I
wanted to hurt him.

The wind stirred the mimosa opposite, almost in sympathy
with him.

He ignored me. "We not, no did not do it, you know. She
always stop me before we . . . It is 'heavy petting.' This is what
you say? Yes?"

I nodded. *Another of his conquests, but why is he telling me?*

"But not—it is all planned. I have no idea—her father. He is
big in government."

"Yeah. So, what? You were set up?" Feeling a wave of sickness coming over me, I stood up. My legs were shaky, but I couldn't show this weakness to Moussa. I made myself carefully walk over to a bench in the shade. The heat had drained my energy. Moussa followed me, muttering and feeling sorry for himself.

"These are powerful people. I could disappear. No one know. They have film of me with her. Me, a little tiny, tiny fish in this shark sea."

I looked up and corrected him. "Shark-infested sea. Go on."

"I am fucked." He sat down next to me. "She lured, yes, lured me into trap like mouse." He looked at me with the sad brown eyes of a puppy, not knowing what to do next.

"What about Farid?" I asked. "His father is FLN, isn't he?"

"Yes. He will help, but he is small fish."

I snorted. This was unreal: An alternative universe. "You were told to seduce me, then Elizabeth?"

"No. No. When I meet. No . . . met you, I didn't . . ." Moussa smiled at himself for using the correct form of to meet. I let him continue. "The police come to me after . . . when I tell the story of Liz and her revenge."

"Oh, it's Liz's fault? Have you told her?"

"No. Do not tell her. I'm so sorry I do this to you. I love you both. Oh, this one big fucking mess."

I laughed at and with Moussa—to relieve the tension. When we had been in the room with Captain Touati, talking about what we should do to entrap JJ, I couldn't help looking at Moussa's soft lips and curly, tousled hair. I felt weak at the knees with a hollow sensation in my stomach—fear or desire?

We sat in silence, blanked out and lost in our own private thoughts. Then a flock of birds, stammering and chattering, burst out of the trees opposite us. I looked up and saw Farid striding across the garden. "I am looking for you. We have to work how Dave is going to meet Jean Jacques."

SEVENTEEN

Back in the heat of Bou Saâda, the sirocco swirled hot Saharan dust at us. During the day, it wasn't pleasant to be outside in the dry, energy-sapping heat. Algerians became nighttime animals, sleeping and dozing in the afternoons and shopping and socializing in the later hours. Like all of us, the French instructors were waiting for the final days of June and our paychecks with the release notice, so we could buy plane tickets. Farid and his father must have "arranged" a special dispensation for Sue and Liz to fly out earlier.

Hugh organized a party at his house overlooking the oued. I don't know what kind of pressure they'd put on him, but it was all part of an Algerian clandestine existence. A couple of months ago, Sue and I had joked about Hugh being an agent for MI6. He was so British public-school. Now I felt maybe it wasn't as far-fetched as we had thought, and it could explain why he had suddenly arranged this convenient little party.

It was simple: I had to meet Jean Jacques, tell him Seamus had given Susan an envelope for safekeeping, arrange to see him at Al Caïd Hotel, and give him the papers.

Hugh invited a mix of instructors and a few Arab friends described as a mixing of cultures: West and East. This allowed Moussa and Farid to be there. I was nervous as hell but clueless as to what Jean Jacques was doing. Thinking about it, I was merely a tiny cog in a vast machine with no sense of purpose except to get this done and then forget about it.

As a host, Hugh was perfect, offering wine to some, soft drinks to others, telling them about the food, and introducing people. He introduced me to JJ, but of course I already knew him. We talked for a minute while Farid played the flute and watched us all.

It was the early evening, and most of us were inside his sitting room. A ceiling fan stirred the hot, dry air, and a few papers waved and flapped, trying to escape. You could feel the gritty wind-blown sand on your skin and even taste it, as a fine coat of dust had settled on the surface of the dark red wine in my glass. It coated everything and smelled of the mysterious deep Sahara.

The double doors to the garden were open, and a few people wandered around or sat on the garden chairs chatting. I could make out some words of the Imam calling prayer time, "*Allah akbar . . . Haya ala s-saleh* (God is great . . . Come to prayer)." The call drifted across the oued–calming and peaceful: Maghrib, the sunset prayer.

Realizing the polite social questions bored Jean Jacques, I said, "Wow, it's hot. I've got to get some fresh air." I leaned closer, "I've got something to tell you about Seamus."

"What?"

"Not here. Come outside for a few minutes." He looked at me and shrugged.

We made our way out onto the balcony overlooking the oued. It was peaceful, but importantly, we were alone. High above the palmeraie, a half-moon threw its pale light over the oued, where a few palm trees swayed in an occasional light wind, caressing them.

"I have something to give you from Seamus."

"Rubbish. He has nothing for me. The police searched your apartment."

"Yes, but Seamus gave an envelope to Susan before he was arrested and told her to keep it for him."

"This is months later. Why now?"

"I didn't know if I could trust you, or if you would be arrested."

Jean Jacques snorted at such a ludicrous suggestion. "Have you opened it?"

This was getting ridiculous: A bit like fishing. I had caught him but now had to reel him in slowly. "No. All I know is Seamus told Susan if anything happened to him, she had to pass it on to you."

"Where is it?"

"Not with me. We can meet later and I'll pass you the envelope."

"Where?"

A man of few words, but I didn't like him or his air of superiority. Looking closely at him, I noticed his angular features—a chiseled chin and a long, bony nose—and because of his height, he looked down at me. He had a disdainful look on his face, and his hard, black eyes gave him the look of a feral animal. I hated myself, but imagining his hostility made me feel comfortable with what I was doing. However, I had to continue.

"Al Caïd Hotel. I'll go there with the envelope and do some marking as cover in the garden." I still sounded a little nervous, likely because of the disdain on his face as he looked at me.

He snapped back, not wasting any words. "Bring a briefcase, get it from the supermarket: black with a handle. I'll bring the same. We will exchange."

"OK. Eight tomorrow night?"

"Seven. You go an hour earlier alone and look busy." More a command than a request.

He had been concise and cutting, and before I could even acknowledge what he had said, he walked back into the party. I watched him walking up the corridor without even saying goodbye. Then I had no real idea about what was happening.

Later, I wondered if Jean Jacques had been testing me, trying to decide if he could trust me or not.

Walking back towards the party, I started feeling giddy and staggered after him but had to hold on to a table to steady myself. My mind whirled with impossible questions. *What was in the envelope the captain had given me? Should I look? Maybe the less you know, the better. Who can I trust? Moussa? Farid? What about him? He's helping his cousin, but his father is FLN. Jean Jacques? Whose side is he on? Which side am I on?* All these thoughts and contradictions confused me. The glasses of wine I had downed didn't calm my nerves. I was on my own and had sold myself out.

Moussa came over to me as I stood watching the table gently shift in and out of focus. "Are you OK, Dave?"

Moussa caught me as I was slipping to the floor. I came around for a few seconds, my head resting on his shoulder while he helped me to walk along the corridor. A bright light shone in my eyes, then darkness. I heard a door open and whispers, but I must have passed out again. Later, I remember being helped out of a car with Moussa and Farid holding me and walking me upstairs. The next time I came to consciousness, I was lying on a mattress with Moussa wiping my face with a wet cloth and Farid looking at me intently. I felt so weak.

"I'm sorry, so sorry. I don't know . . . What happened? Where am I?"

"At home. Did he agree with meet you?" Moussa asked.

I looked blankly at him. My head still revolving. "Who?"

"Jean Jacques. Did he agree meet you in hotel tomorrow?"

"Oh." I tried to think back. "Yes . . ."

"At eight?" Moussa snapped out, his penetrating brown eyes showing his desperation.

My head was foggy, and I felt confused. I struggled to recall the conversation. "I think JJ said that."

Farid muttered in Arabic, got up and left.

When I woke in the morning, the bright sunlight was so intense I shut my eyes, trying to ease the throbbing in my head and the aches all over my body. Moussa got up and returned with a glass of fizzing water, which I drank gratefully.

"Were you here all night?" I asked him a little incredulously, shaking my head to clear the fog.

"Yes," he replied.

"Why?"

"I want to make sure you not . . . be sick." He was showing his caring, soft side. "You remember the words Jean Jacques say?"

"Jean Jacques? Yes. Not happy. We have to meet in the Al Caïd Hotel garden. Six, or seven?"

"OK. We go at seven. Well, no, six, in case. Now, I make some coffee. You get up. Farid want see you."

He left the room. *Who is he?* I remembered Farid watching me when I had surfaced from a coma-like state, like a doctor observing a patient for his vital signs.

I hadn't drunk that much wine, had I? One of the glasses tasted different. Drugged? Who could it have been? Jean Jacques' people? Farid? He'd been playing the flute and watching me. The effort of getting up made the room swirl. I lay down again and groaned.

EIGHTEEN

I woke hours later and stumbled into the bathroom to throw water from the bath over myself. In the kitchen, I found Moussa and Farid laughing and joking, but they stopped when I entered.

"What's going on? Talking about me?"

"No, sorry, Dave. We have other things we talk, not only you." Moussa had an engaging, sweet expression: the-butter-wouldn't-melt kind of look. "We surprised you are awake. How are you?"

"Awful, like a hangover from drinking. I think the wine I drank had been drugged. I've never done that before."

Moussa quickly replied, "It was heat and wine. You're not used. Not like we? Us? You not like us Arabs."

Farid looked at me, increasing my anxiety. I gulped some of the coffee Moussa had brought for me, giving me time to recover, then I looked at him again.

Farid pressed on with his questions, "What else do you remember Jean Jacques said?"

"Oh yes, something about getting a briefcase from the supermarket. To swap."

"OK. We have time before meeting tonight," Moussa said. "Let's go for walk up Kardada. You show me where you take Liz."

"Isn't it too hot?"

"Almost 3 o'clock. It will get cooler. You don't go before six."

"Is Farid coming too?" I asked, thinking I'd like to be alone with Moussa for a while.

"No, he will buy briefcase. Come. Let's go."

Stumbling, we crossed the oued, clambering up the rock-strewn hillside until we reached the top. Higher up, the wind was refreshing, and it felt good to be cooled by the rushing air. As we scrambled up the rocky slope, trying hard not to twist our ankles and breathing heavily from the exertion, I croaked out a question. "Why were you laughing when I came into the kitchen?"

"Oh, nothing. We laughing when you falling, and I catch you. Before, I give you mild sedative."

"What?" I asked angrily, sucking in air to fill my bursting lungs and rest my pounding heart. "Why?"

"We need excuse to leave party together."

"Bloody hell." *Once again, I've been left out of decisions.* "You could have told me."

"Sorry. We . . . Look, enjoy view of mountains."

We had reached the top, and I hobbled, exhausted, over the sharp-edged rocks to Eagle's Point. I was still angry at Moussa but felt exhilarated standing on the rock platform and feeling the up-current of air pulling and tugging at my shirt. I took it off and let the wind cool my skin. It felt liberating. I looked down at the shimmering river and wanted to fly. Moussa came and stood next to me, took off his shirt and together, we braced against the buffeting wind. "Look at the river. The mountains. It's incredible. It makes you feel insignificant. Don't you feel it?"

"Yes. It is incredible." He put his arm around me as we braced against the wind. "I cannot let anything happen for you, Dave."

Can I believe him? His arm around me felt so comforting and safe. I was alone—both Sue and Liz had gone—and maybe it was part of the plan. I didn't know what to do, but I had to trust someone.

He turned and kissed me with a surprising fervor and intensity. "I love you both."

"I know. I feel the same."

Moussa grinned and shouted into the wind, "Love."

We sang a few lines of the Beatles' song, laughing and feeling totally content.

"Does Liz know about us?"

"No, I do not think that," he replied, then asked the same question. "Does Susan know?"

"I don't know. She might think something is . . ." I shrugged. It didn't really matter. Was I conflicted? I'm not sure if I even needed to go there. I felt free—aware that happiness is where you find it. My feelings for Moussa were just as strong as my feelings for Sue, and I needed them both to be complete. What did that mean? A better question would be: Am I betraying Sue? I had told her about my affair with Steve. Moussa was like a beautiful bird that would fly away. I knew that but I couldn't stop loving and wanting him.

Our heads touched, and we kissed—a soft, lingering kiss full of possibilities, but we had to leave to prepare for the hotel handover.

◆ ◆ ◆

When Farid handed me the briefcase, I asked him directly, "What about Jean Jacques? What's his role in this?"

Farid looked uncomfortable. He looked at Moussa, who smiled nervously.

"What aren't you telling me?"

Farid took a deep breath. "You cannot talk about this. You signed that paper, remember? With Touati? If you tell people—we can't help you."

This was becoming unfathomable. *Farid? What does he know?*

"I need to know what's happening." I felt under pressure and panicky.

"We are trying to get Jean Jacques to . . ."

"To what? Why are you involved?"

"I've told you, my father, he is FLN. He knows everything. It's an agreement to . . ."

He suddenly stopped, realizing he had said too much.

"An agreement to do what, Farid?"

Moussa leaned over to Farid and said something in Arabic to him.

"My father, he told me what to do," Farid said quietly. "We need Jean Jacques to help us find other men."

"What?" I sat down and looked in disbelief at Farid. "Then why was he so difficult?"

"He test you. See if he can trust you." My head was spinning. *Why hadn't they told me? What is going on?*

"He needs to show he has contacts." He paused and then let it all out. "The people Jean Jacques know are planning coup against our government. They want to replace president with one more friendly with French."

I looked at Farid with disbelief. If true, this was incredible: unbelievable.

"So, what's all this handing over of papers for?" I asked.

"Money and papers, to show Jean Jacques is on their side. Someone in French embassy gave the envelope to Seamus. Maybe they thought an Irishman would be . . . more easy."

"So why couldn't you tell me?"

"We did not know if we could . . .? If you would do it." Farid said quietly.

"Farid, why did they deport Seamus?"

Farid looked at me. I suppose he was calculating how much he could tell me. "They did not trust him, and . . . They needed. . . . They wanted someone who . . . someone we . . . You are friends with Moussa. He is my cousin. We know you are a good man."

"What's your role in this, Farid?" I asked, even though I was shocked to know he was so involved.

"I tell my father what is happening."

"What about Moussa?" I wanted to know about his role in this.

"It's time," Moussa said. "We have to go. We can talk later."

NINETEEN

As we drove down to Al Caïd Hotel, I thought about how much both Moussa and I had changed. These last few days, I'd become suspicious, trapped in this pantomime. I was playing a small part in a bigger picture, rather like an extra in a play: the spear-carrier, without a speaking role, but still essential to provide colour.

As an actor, I knew exactly how to play my part. I'd been a walk-on all my life—yes, in plays, but also in aspects of life. I never played a major role, always letting others lead, so I might as well continue doing what I know best. All I had to do was look the part of a teacher marking his papers, talking in a friendly way, and murmuring "rhubarb-rhubarb" in the background for only a few minutes to establish a veneer of friendship. Then JJ could get up, pick up the other briefcase, and leave. I would stay a little longer, sip my beer, pack up my papers, and walk out too: the end of my participation in this drama.

Words like *pantomime* and *farce* brought me back to life. I had to take this more seriously. I remembered what I had been taught: every role had to be played to perfection. You had to believe absolutely in what you were doing; otherwise, there was no reality. It didn't matter how small a role you had if you acted it genuinely.

"This is one crazy thing to do." Fear once again took over. It was the gut-wrenching hole in my stomach, the feeling you want to piss and vomit at the same time that overwhelmed me: stage fright.

Moussa touched me on my shoulder. "Come on. It's OK. There are much people in hotel. No one will do anything. Police are there."

"OK," I said, "Let's do this . . ." I clenched my fists to make me concentrate. The show must go on.

Al Caïd Hotel was lit up to accentuate its fortress-like appearance. The white walls towered above me, and the shadows were dark and severe. It was imposing. With rounded towers on each side, the gatehouse led visitors directly toward the entrance where two large arched wooden doors stood open.

I walked into the deep shadow for a few seconds, following the light pulling me into a brightly lit lobby. The contrast between the massive exterior walls and the brightly coloured reception desk was a shock: designed no doubt to welcome the guests to the modern world after traversing a medieval Arabian fable. I turned left and entered the jasmine-scented garden, ordering a beer as I passed the bar. The fragrance hung sweetly in the air, and I greedily breathed it in to refresh and cleanse my lungs of the arid, dry air outside this creation of paradise. I remembered jasmine had welcomed me to this town so long ago. *I had travelled so far from that night. If the bus hadn't been late, how much of this would have played out? None. Fate plays tricks with you. I'd been drawn into a web of intrigue, and yet . . . Yet, I'd met Moussa. My life, and all our lives, had been changed. It would have been easier, but this is living a life I'd never have dreamed of.* Water trickled from fountains and dribbled down rocky slopes to tinkle and splash in the pools below. It made the air fresh and more breathable. Refreshed, I was ready.

The Friday night diners were drinking and gossiping before dinner. I noticed quite a few tourists and some businessmen dressed in suits and a general air of relaxation. Choosing a table with my back to the wall, I sat down. A youthful, striking waiter opened the bottle and poured a little into my glass. He smiled directly at me and gave me a secret little wiggle of his eyebrows. I thanked him. *Was that a signal? Was he secret police?*

Downing the first few gulps of ice-cooled beer, I felt better. Beer was hard to get outside of the capital and the big tourist hotels, so this was a treat. I poured a little more into the glass with surprisingly steady hands, creating a small head of foam. A couple of mouthfuls left me feeling confident and gave me the determination to continue. Putting the glass down, I sorted my papers and then placed my briefcase on the floor beside the chair on my right. *Better not to overthink. Play the role and be convincing.* Reading a paper one of my private students had written for me, I occasionally made a mark or wrote a comment with a red pen. Immersed in my marking, I was surprised by a greeting in English by a French speaker.

"Good evening, Dave. *Ça va?*"

I looked up into Jean Jacques' angular features and forced a smile. "*Oui. Tout va bien. Et vous? Ça va?*"

"*Oui.*" He switched to English, perhaps so we wouldn't be overheard and understood by too many people. "Can I join you for a few minutes?"

"Yes, of course. Sit down." He sat down and put his briefcase on the ground next to mine. "Would you like a beer? *Garçon. Une bière, s'il vous plaît.*"

We were both playing our parts wonderfully well. *Maybe I do get to have a few lines in this, after all.* We chatted about inconsequential things. The waiter placed a second bottle and glass on the table and returned to the bar. I told JJ that I was marking some papers for a private student and asked him about his holiday plans. The normal chit-chat.

As we were talking, a man about the same age as Jean Jacques approached, and immediately my heartbeat increased. *Is JJ playing a trick?* I looked at him as he stopped in front of us. *"Bonsoir, Jean Jacques." JJ knows him? He's French, fashionable clothes, short hair, military?*

JJ stood up and greeted him. *"Bonsoir, Phillipe. Ca va?"* They shook hands, smiling and obviously pleased to see each other. JJ introduced me, and I stood up to shake hands. *A contact? Does he have a gun? A knife?* As we're shaking hands, I'm thinking: *He's got a knife.*

Nothing happened.

I sat down, sweating. *This was totally out of script.* JJ looked relaxed, and they chatted away in French, ignoring me. I couldn't catch much of what they said, as they spoke in dialect. *So I wouldn't understand? Are they laughing at me?* Phillipe looked at me with the crooked smile of a jackal. "You are English? And friends with Jean Jacques?"

"Um, yes we . . . umm, we teach in the same school." *I'm so fucking nervous I can hardly speak.*

"Are you alright? You look a little red?"

"No, I'm fine. Sorry." *Why are you apologizing?* "Maybe it's the heat and beer." I swept my hand over the table and knocked JJ's bottle over. Beer spread quickly across the table, flooding my student's papers, and they greedily soaked up the alcohol.

"Sorry. Sorry." *Shut up, you fucking moron.*

"Dave, Phillipe and I are going. Stay, err finish your marking." Jean Jacques smirked at the mess my student's papers were in. *God, he's so smug.* Without offering to clear up, he swapped briefcases, said, *"Bonne soirée,"* and the two of them walked out of the garden.

What a fucking disaster. I had to breathe slowly to calm down. The waiter came over, mopped up the beer, and asked if I wanted another one.

"No," I answered in English, my brain shutting down.

My hands shaking, I picked up the ruined papers, grabbed JJ's briefcase, got up and walked, head held high, to my car.

At last, sitting in a safe place. I pounded the steering wheel, releasing the fear and anger. The pain helped.

Breathing slowly, a wave of relief swept over me. *I'd done it. Apart from the beer bottle, it all went smoothly. They can worry about Phillipe. Not my problem. Double my salary.*

I regained a sense of myself and drove to the centre of town.

TWENTY

The silence of the square was in marked contrast to the intrigue I had been involved in. It had gone well, and it had taken less than five minutes. A solitary car drove past, its lights cutting into the darkness. The few streetlights provided worlds of dull yellow. Flying ants, attracted and confused, flew madly around these pools of false daylight.

I had been invited for dinner at Moussa's house. After carefully observing the square, I picked up a plastic bag, got out of the car, and locked the door. The overwhelming aroma of roasting meat and wood smoke permeated the still night air. A barbecue. We would eat well tonight. Walking towards his house, I felt content with the world. I knew they wouldn't be there yet, but it had been arranged that a student of mine, Mustafa, would greet me.

It was an imposing house, now faded, and the paint on the walls was peeling, but still an impressive relic of colonial days when the French ruled this outpost of their empire. Merchants and farmers had made vast profits from growing wheat, wine, and dates to sell into the world markets. The faded glory of their houses reflected their wealth. I raised a hefty brass hand holding a ball and let it thud twice on the thick wood-panelled door.

Mustafa opened the door. "Teacher. Welcome. Come in."

"Thank you, Mustafa. I'm a little early, I think."

"No, no. Do not worry. Moussa come back soon. He get Farid."

I handed him the plastic bag, and the bottles inside clinked satisfactorily. "Something for our dinner."

"Thank you, teacher. Come in."

The little charade at the front door had been rehearsed in case anyone was watching or taking note of my arrival. He led me into the *majlis*, the Arab sitting room, and to Captain Touati.

"David, welcome. How did it go?"

"Good, no problem. Oh, JJ met a guy called Phillipe. He came to the table." *Best be upfront about it.*

"Yes, I heard. We know him. Do not worry. Thank you, Dave. You have done a service to Algeria."

Mustafa handed the captain the plastic bag. After extracting the two bottles of wine, he pulled out the briefcase JJ had swapped with me and quickly opened it to peer inside.

"Well, you have a lot to celebrate. This will not be forgotten, Dave."

Moussa and Farid walked in, grinning and looking pleased with themselves. "It went well. We watch from room upstairs and wait for other guests leave. No one see us. Well done, Dave."

"Yes," said Farid. "It went well."

Are they not going to mention Phillipe, or have they already briefed him? Probably told to cheer me up.

"Right. I will leave by the back door. *Bon appetit.*"

"Oh, sir." I wanted to flatter his ego.

"Oh, come on, Dave. Call me Walid."

"Walid, can I ask a question?"

The captain laughed a little and coughed lightly. "Oh, I forget. Tickets for you and Moussa. I nearly leave with them." He handed over my ticket and gave Moussa his. "You are both on same flight to London. Only business class, all other seats booked." As he said this, he smirked, "Oh yes, your contracts: Sue, Liz, and yours. You should find them satisfactory."

We thanked him again, said our goodbyes, and he left.

"Wow."

Moussa interrupted and said, "Dave, I've got one question for you."

"Go ahead."

"Are you come back next year?"

"Yes, I love working here, and now it's all over, we can have a normal life again. Sue wants to return, too. She said if it all went well, then, of course, we would come back. And, to tell the truth, the money is good."

◆ ◆ ◆

His mother, as usual, had prepared an excellent meal. The aroma of lamb roasting on a spit in the courtyard was intoxicating in itself, eaten this time with a mound of rice. To follow Arab custom, you had to ball it up in your right hand and flick it into your mouth without spilling too many grains. I wasn't very adept at it and soon had a pile of rice by my feet as we sat cross-legged on a carpet in the middle of the room with a large bowl of rice and the roasted lamb placed on top. Pieces of meat and other delicacies were tossed in front of me as a gesture of friendship to ensure I got the best bits.

We drank the wine, and after eating, Moussa played some early Beatles records. It was relaxing and pleasant, with all the tension of the early evening erased in the company of friends.

Around eleven, I left to drive back to my flat, and Moussa walked with me to my car. It was a dark night, no moon, and the few electric streetlights gave a low glow. The insects were still crazily flying around in circles, attracted by the mock sun.

Then I noticed an outline of what could have been a man, half in the shadows created by one of the lights. It moved a little. *Are we being watched?* I mentioned it to Moussa, but he laughed and said, "You are dreaming."

I looked again—nothing. It was possible, I suppose, and maybe the wine was making me imagine things that didn't exist.

"I come with you," Moussa said. "I don't like you be on your own."

"No. It's OK. Thanks."

"Not good answer, Dave. Give me keys." He spoke in a forceful, don't-argue-with-me kind of voice.

I handed them to him. Actually, I didn't want to be on my own tonight, realizing it was our last night together and that I could do with Moussa's company and protection.

With a naughty, boyish grin, he said, "Maybe we have some fun as well."

"Maybe," I said, smirking back.

We flew out on the last day of June. Settling back into my seat in business class beside Moussa, I looked forward to an almost three-month break visiting California. With a bonus of a few thousand pounds in my bank, we could really enjoy ourselves.

It was over and hadn't been nearly as bad as my imagination had created. All the intrigue forgotten, I leaned back in my seat and relaxed.

Hugh's comments about staying in Algeria resurfaced. "It's the light, the sun's warmth, the freshness and purity of the air, and the aesthetic beauty of the desert."

But it's also the comfort of friends and the feeling you belong.

PART TWO

ONE

Sue and I had met Moussa and Liz in London for the last five days of the holiday. We rented a flat near Westbourne Park tube station. A great location near Notting Hill, and Kensington High Street only a bus ride away. We were still spending the money we'd made in our last year in Algeria, and it felt great to go out shopping and to eat in some of the best restaurants in the area or just to cook in the flat. We were on a permanent high, enjoying being together and loving the innocence of life and peace away from the intrigue of the previous year.

The late summer heat hit us as the hostess opened the aircraft doors. We'd left a cold, wet, windy London and then sat in economy for five hours on Air Algerie, wedged in our seats. Sue and I looked up at the blue skies welcoming us and beamed.

Breathing in the air of Algeria, even on the tarmac, the overriding essence of jet fuel was tempered with a light salty breeze blowing up from the sea. Upon entering the Immigration and Customs Hall, the malfunctioning air-conditioning circulated the sweat of close-contact human bodies.

Farid met us and, using his contacts, guided us effortlessly through passport control and customs. Visas stamped and luggage checked, we entered the hustle and seeming chaos outside the

110

airport. The shouting and gesticulating with offers of taxis or hotels brought the real world back into focus. We had returned: now for year two.

Algiers in the evening teemed with street life. We had booked a hotel near the old quarter, and Moussa and Farid showed us around the main square at the bottom and then up the steep and winding paths leading into the ancient town. As we climbed, the lights below portrayed a magical city that didn't seem to sleep.

Here in the old quarter, with the dim streetlights and thick wooden doors on Arab houses keeping the outside world at a distance, it was all so private and calm. The smell of the sea and the wood smoke from the barbecues grilling fish and kebabs of skewered meat wafted up from the square. We descended again and watched people strolling, sitting at café tables, and hurrying past to meetings with friends. The guttural calls of Arabic welcomed us back to a now-familiar world.

"Let's hope this year will be easier and less dramatic," I said to the friends wandering with me.

"Oh, I forgot to tell you. I have been accepted at Algiers University to study English. I want to be translator. Work for UN or something." Farid said, smiling and looking at us for a comment.

"I'm so pleased for you, Farid," said Elizabeth, and the rest of us joined in congratulating him. "Where will you be staying?"

"Oh, with Moussa. He has a house now. We live together and go to university. You can come and visit us at weekends."

"We always enjoy coming to Algiers. Thank you."

Sue then brought up the question we all wanted to ask but hadn't dared to. "What happened to Jean Jacques?"

"I don't know," said Farid. "I have not heard about him."

"Really?" asked Elizabeth incredulously.

"It's probably good not to talk here in square."

"And Beau?"

"We will talk later."

Not knowing bothered us, we knew he wasn't going to tell us much, but as we'd been involved in no small way, we felt entitled to know. We had tried to discuss this with Moussa in London, but he said he really didn't know.

On the plane, Moussa had mentioned he wanted us to get together and winked at me in a knowing, come-on way. As he looked me in the eyes, my desire for him stirred. I also speculated about what Farid hadn't told us in the square and why he was concerned about someone overhearing, but I reckoned we would be told something tomorrow.

A light breeze off the Mediterranean cooled the evening air, and Farid and Moussa left, promising they'd be back in the morning. We returned to our hotel, where Sue opened the window. Street sounds poured in: car horns, a radio playing a lilting Egyptian ballad, and the rhythmic flapping of a flag.

Sue was strong-minded and loved the beauty and stimulation Algeria gave her. Having already spent a couple of years here before meeting me, Susan knew more than me about the politics of both Algerian and French attitudes. Politically, she supported the underdog, the downtrodden, and the poor who didn't have a voice.

When I had first seen her sitting at the café table with the young Frenchmen, I'd thought one of them was her boyfriend. She liked discussing things in French and was fluent, whereas I had a patois French. However, she later told me she'd had enough of their French ways, especially after her divorce from her French husband.

Susan had invited me to have sex with her. She'd thought I was gay because of Steve, but it was a test I had passed. However, at the time, I didn't know how much she knew about my relationship with Moussa.

On holiday, we'd gone camping—driving around California and sleeping on the ground visiting Anza-Borrego, Yosemite, and other national parks—a carefree, easy time.

Sue was older than me and had been married before. During our time camping, she told me about her life with her first husband and her time in Paris and Algeria.

One night we sat around a campfire, listening to the crackling of the wood and watching the flames flicker and dance into the sky. Sue talked about her earlier life and I listened, enthralled.

"Coming from L.A. and being in Paris was exciting. I roamed the streets of the Latin Quarter and along the banks of the Seine, and on one of those evening walks, I met Michel. He was good-looking with the added value of French charm. I'd never met anyone like him back in California. He treated me to dinners, and we walked everywhere, stopping in cafes, going to the museums, meeting and talking with people on the street. So much more exciting and alive than anything I knew back in L.A. When Michel asked me to marry him and go to Algeria with him, I accepted. The chance of a lifetime."

I looked up at the vast expanse of sky above us and made out Orion striding his way across the heavens. I loved listening to Sue talk, and I pressed her to continue. She stared into the fire, mesmerized by the flames.

"We lived in a villa with its feet in the Med at the end of a long, curving, sandy beach. I woke every morning to the swishing of the sea, watched the sunrise, drank my coffee, and ate freshly baked croissants, luxuriating in the early morning light."

"Sounds really great." I poured a second glass of California Chablis and passed one to Sue. "Tell me what you did. Where? Annaba?"

"Yes. A beautiful city. I had a lot of free time and took the car out for drives into the countryside. Discovering ruined Roman cities where you could wander along empty streets, imagining how it must have been."

When we had first met, Sue had talked about Algeria and her life there. I knew she had been married, but she had never talked much about him. "Tell me about Michel."

"Michel had affairs. They all did, only I didn't know. The ex-pat French would get together, do French things, talk politics, gossip, eat long, slow meals, smoke, talk again, and swap partners—an open-house on sexual freedom. It shocked me, all these wife-swapping parties and the number of married men who had mistresses, often another man's wife. My upbringing hadn't been puritanical, but living in Algeria, it seemed no rules applied. I soon realized what a bastard and two-timing prick my husband was. He wasn't interested in me. He just wanted to bed as many women as he could."

"I found out he was having an affair with his yoga teacher, Marie Claire. One morning, she demanded the group get up early and drive to a remote spot overlooking the Mediterranean. He told me when he returned in the morning what they had done. High up on a cliff face overlooking the Mediterranean Sea, they'd greeted the sun and performed yoga. She'd hooked him, and he didn't bother to hide it." Sue paused, finished her glass, and reached for more. I could see tears in her eyes.

To cheer her up, I said, "I'm so happy to have met you. Let's drink a toast to our life together." We clinked glasses. "If you want to go on. I'm listening."

"He described what they had done. They had sat naked facing the sea. He told me they were caressed by the uplifting currents of air, gathering the energy force from the sea and the near-vertical cliff below them." Sue guffawed. "Michel didn't talk like that; he was under the spell of Marie Claire."

I nodded and shrugged. When we first met, Sue had talked about some of this, but it seemed she added more details each time she told me. Embellishing or just remembering?

"The fool told me about doing yoga to greet the sun with the golden rays gently caressing his body. I mean, can you believe it? I remembered his actual words. I wrote them down so I could throw them back at him."

I let her continue. I could tell she was still disturbed by this two, no, three years later. But being with Sue was such an enlightening experience for me. She had passion, anger, and love all rolled up into one. The fire crackled and spat out sparks of light, reminding me that we still existed in this present.

"Go on," I said. "What did Michel say?" She had never reached this point in her storytelling. *What could Michel, the infamous seducer of women, have said to make Sue so mad she still carried this anger?*

"He told me it was incredible and arousing. The *salo* remarked he felt at peace and harmony communing with *nature au naturel*. Naked as the day he was born." Sue grimaced, and I snorted derision to show support for her.

She continued by mimicking Michel, describing what they had done. "'Standing on the cliff above the sea, we all did The Tree Pose to welcome the rising sun, humming in harmony and drawing strength from its welcoming rays. Then the Dog Pose.' I screamed 'stop!' but he said, 'You must come next time.'"

I laughed at the absurdity of it all. By mocking him, I hoped she had discovered a degree of equilibrium.

"The second summer, Michel ran off with her. He lied and told me he had a business trip to Algiers, but I knew. I was so sick of his duplicity."

I had long since run out of words to say. I wanted to soothe her, but Sue was lost in painful memories. I let the silence of the night close in around us, and like a balm it pacified her. Then an owl hooted, and as it flew over us, we felt the softness and gentle caress of its wingbeats.

Eventually, I cut through the peacefulness of the night air with, "He's a bastard. Forget him. He's not worth it." Not original, but what else could I say? It stirred Sue to finish.

She was calmer now, "You're right. He came back two weeks later—tail between his legs. Marie Claire had dumped him. We had blazing rows, and over the next few months, it became impossible to live there."

I'd stupidly stirred up her passion again, and her voice was cracking with emotion.

"It was hard to leave the villa and Algeria, but we divorced. I left and flew to the UK. I was alone again, and quite honestly, I don't do well when I am alone. I tried doing part-time typing jobs, but the idea of doing that for years appalled me. The cold, wet, long days of winter with low clouds blocking out the sun were depressing. I dreamt of returning to Algeria, and walking the hills with the scents of lavender, heather, and wild garlic. Heaven compared to the purgatory of London. The one thing I learned is not to be jealous. It ruins lives."

◆ ◆ ◆

Sue and I made love our first night back in Algeria, and it was more passionate than it had been for quite a while. What was so stimulating about Algeria? All the pheromones floating through the open window? The swaggering guys on the street with their sexual magnetism?

We had our breakfast outside at a small café table: hot, strong coffee, warm croissants with butter and honey, and a crusty French baguette. Moussa and Farid sat with us, and we talked about Algeria, our holidays, and what we could do for the next few days before heading south to start teaching again.

Farid and Moussa exchanged glances, and Moussa nodded. Then Farid said, "OK, and now for news about Jean Jacques. We are in briefing with Captain Touati last night. I must tell you. It is not finished yet."

"What?" I screamed, spraying a jet of coffee over the table. "Sorry," I blurted out in between bouts of coughing.

"What do you mean?" interjected Susan, but I continued to splutter and grabbed a glass of water to clear my throat. "Stop making a spectacle of yourself."

Farid waited until I had recovered, smiled sympathetically at me, and then said, "No, not yet. The police watch them and looking . . . are looking for evidence. Touati wants to give you briefing tonight."

"Oh, no. No. No. No. We've done our share," Susan said aggressively. Liz agreed, and I nodded, inwardly dreading what Farid would say next. And quite honestly, I'd had nagging doubts it really was all over.

A fluffy cumulus cloud cast a momentary shadow over our table. Seagulls cackled, trying to calculate if they could snatch some of the bread lying uneaten on our plates. People walked past, unaware of our anguish. Life continued as usual. Our naivety in thinking we were getting all this money for nothing came crashing home: The bonus was a payment for extra services.

"OK. What do we need to know?" I asked, dreading the answer. "It's also interesting you said they need us . . . but not you two?"

Moussa put his hand out to stop Farid from speaking, and then he said gently, "No, we all in this. You must do meeting with Jean Jacques. You know exchange. Like before. You work in same school, so it OK you are friends."

I looked around the square and noticed a group of young men two tables across from us. They were arguing loudly, probably discussing last night's game. One of them glanced across at me. He had the usual garb of jeans and a tight T-shirt, bulging biceps and glistening skin. His eyes flashed a lustful longing. But then I realized he wasn't looking at me, but at Liz and her golden hair.

She shook it, and her hair cascaded onto her bare shoulders. I shrugged it off and forgot about it until the guys got up and passed by our table. As he strutted past, Lustful muttered, "*Je suis beau, non?*" Moussa rose as if to go after him, but Farid restrained him.

Sue leaned across to me and muttered, "When I get you back to the room tonight. I'm going to give you a good spanking."

I grinned. A spanking sounded fun. I leaned back to whisper, "Why, what have I done?"

She replied in a sweet sexy murmur. "You know."

Trying to recover my composure, I returned my thoughts to the group sitting at the table. "OK. OK. I get it, but I need a break from all this spy and intrigue stuff. So, we intend to visit our friends in Hadjout and go to Tipaza and the beach again."

Farid shrugged, "You are free until tonight. Do what you like."

"Oh, well, thank you very much," I said somewhat sarcastically. "Our masters are letting us have a few hours of normality. Sue and I have already arranged to go. You can come if you want. It's a wonderful place."

"I can't," said Moussa, "but Liz, you can go. Meeting Captain Touati. Tonight, eight—same hotel."

"Right." I wanted to know what we were expected to do, but it could all wait. "Are you OK? Sue? Liz?"

Sue agreed by nodding her head, but she didn't look too happy about it.

Liz looked at Moussa and shrugged. "OK," she said, "we might as well get some time off before heading back into this spy world of yours, Moussy."

I'd heard her pet name for him before. It always made me smile, and I'm sure Moussa coloured as she said it.

TWO

Tipaza is beautiful. The village has a small harbour with houses and shops spreading away from the sea and clustered along the bay. More impressive are the ruins of the ancient port of Tipaza at the edge of the town. The Phoenicians created it—a small port for trade—then the Romans, recognizing its strategic value, occupied it. The seaport of Tipaza became one of the major harbours on the Mediterranean coast.

It was a perfect day—clear blue sky, aquamarine sea, hot granite rocks, tall fragrant flowers, and towering shade-giving trees.

We walked down a column-lined street to the sea, where the Mediterranean waves lapped peacefully onto the rocks. It is always fascinating to explore, especially the partially restored amphitheatre. Tall trees provided shade, and wildflowers and gorse grew on the slopes above the crumbled rocks and ancient walls. The air was fresh and a soft breeze gently touched and cooled us.

Algerian families were having a Friday picnic among the ruins. We refused their kind invites to sit down and eat with them. But once or twice, we took the offered homemade baklava, enjoying the sweetness of honey, the flaky pastry, and the pistachio nuts crumbled into the filling. *"Mumtaz, shukran."* Excellent, thank you.

We had lunch at our favourite place: a little wooden shack with a slatted, palm-leafed roof, situated right at the entrance to the Roman ruins. It was immensely pleasurable to sit outside one of the most magnificent Roman sites in North Africa and listen to the sounds of life: a motorbike passing, birds calling and scolding, and chatter in Arabic—as the cook murmured with the only other customer, an Algerian in a brown burnoose with a yellow scarf wrapped around his head. We feasted on steak and fries, finishing off with crepes and jam. This was a far cry from the world of Bou Saâda, where everything was aggressive and hard-edged. Here, the warmth and light calmed and soothed the soul. We sat and reveled in the simple pleasures of life in a state of peacefulness. There was no need to speak. We just relaxed and enjoyed the afternoon light, the quiet, and the utter contentment of being together in a stunningly beautiful setting.

As we were leaving, a youngish man wearing a heavy bernous and a hood over his head dashed out of a side-street shouting and gesticulating. Hooded man saw us and swore in French, "*Putain de merde.*" *Was it directed at us, or just a comment on the general situation he was in?*

He ran past the wooden shack. Two gendarmes with guns drawn rushed past us and grabbed him, knocked him to the ground, and then dragged him along the road and out of sight. It had happened so quickly we hadn't had time to react or even think. Then suddenly, the shock kicked in, and Liz collapsed. A family rushed over to us, apologizing and crying over Liz. They gave her some water and kept repeating, "*Il est fou, ce type. Il est fou.*" He's mad that guy. He's mad.

A senior gendarme jumped out of a passing patrol car and started asking questions and then apologizing. He switched to English, realizing we weren't French, impressing me with his command of the language. "He is crazy man. Not important. Not worry. Nothing is wrong."

We were shaken up but just wanted to leave. It was getting too emotional and intense. So, first thanking the small group of well-wishers that had gathered, I told the officer, "Captain.

I understand. It is OK. We are not making a complaint. We are going to see our friends in Hadjout. Thank you for helping."

Luckily, a Peugeot taxi passed by. The captain stopped it, and we bundled in with him wishing us a safe journey and repeating over and over that nothing was wrong. "Algeria peaceful country."

◆ ◆ ◆

The taxi driver didn't speak during the short ride to the town of Hadjout. But our sense of safety had been shattered. It had been a minor, almost inconsequential incident. Still, we weren't sure if it was just an isolated event or symptomatic of extensive unrest.

As we drove through the town, I noticed the recently built *batiment* (apartment buildings) littered with rubbish and with gangs of unemployed young men loitering outside. They laughed as some of the younger boys tossed rocks into the road and then ran to hide. It wasn't a big deal, but I remembered Cameron had talked about the high unemployment rate in the North. It wasn't as noticeable in the South, but here I felt an air of menace: a pot waiting to boil over. He told us about petty crimes, theft, and menacing behaviour, like following single female teachers, throwing stones at them, and making lewd comments.

Violence hadn't broken out, but the tension and the desire for something better lingered in the streets. However, Sue reminded us of how concerned and helpful the people had been, as they didn't want us to think badly of Algeria. It could have happened anywhere, so we had to put it into perspective. In our experience, we had always been treated with friendliness and hospitality.

For us, a visit to Hadjout was a way to renew ourselves and to escape Bou Saâda's tension, stress, and intrigue. Josephine and Cameron's apartment had luxuries we could only dream of in Bou Saâda: a fridge, running water, a kitchen table with four chairs.

They had made a few good friends. Josephine had a private seventeen-year-old student, and he had introduced them to his family. On Fridays, after prayers, they would often be invited to have an evening meal. Ramzi, Josephine's student, was charming but would be seen as over the top in the UK; but in Algeria, hosts treated their guests and friends well.

"Why not you go ride tomorrow?" Ramzi suggested. "I am working, but a friend, Ramli, work at stables. He have horses."

Josephine tutted and looked at Ramzi. He stopped for a second. "Sorry, he has horses. You can ride on beach like cowboys."

"Yeah, but what if there was another madman . . .?" I asked.

Ramzi laughed. "Oh, come on. One thing to stop you enjoy life? He is mad man. You don't have this in England?"

"Yes, I know. What do you think, Sue? Liz?"

"I can't, I'm afraid. I have to meet someone in Algiers," Liz informed us. I nodded and smiled at her.

Sue laughed. "Let's go. I want to go riding. Thank you, Ramzi. You too?" Sue looked at Cameron and Josephine, and they both nodded.

"OK. Let's do it. I need a change."

We arranged to meet at their flat at eight in the morning. I was pleased because it would take us away from all this undercover work, and you can't live your life afraid of every little thing.

We had the briefing in the evening. Moussa had insisted I came an hour earlier so we could talk about what to expect. When I arrived, he took me to his room, explaining he'd told Liz to go shopping with Sue, so we had the place to ourselves for an hour.

As we entered, Moussa turned around to face me. Standing very close, he looked at me and said quite softly, "I've missed you, Dave. I've missed you too much. I want be alone with you— sit and chat about life."

I looked into his intensely soft and enticing eyes. "Yes, that would be nice."

He opened the doors to the balcony and brought out a few bottles of cold Tango. A light lager, but I'd developed a taste for it. It wasn't easy to get, but the hotel stocked it, so why not enjoy life a little? We were alone, delighting in the breeze, and we relaxed, chatting about our holidays and watching the setting sun create a pool of reflection over the bay.

Then Moussa mentioned the briefing, "Captain Touati will talk on plot to replace Chadli. Some people do not support new President. In French papers, you see anti-Algerian stories for oil and gas contracts. People think French want more easy President."

"Yes, I've heard that, but you're not sure?"

"This group. 'Resist,' meet *Pieds-Noirs* at Marseilles. They make contact with Berber groups here in Algeria and France."

Needing time to process this, I reached for another bottle of Tango. Relishing the coolness of the lager slipping down my throat, I realized this might be more dangerous and far-reaching than I had thought. I hadn't been following the news about Algeria. Over the holiday, we'd been camping and read very little in the papers about it.

I carefully poured some more beer, put the bottle down on the glass-topped table, and looked up at Moussa, who was half-smiling and squinting at the harbour below us.

"From what I know," I said, "there is a lot of ill feeling between the Kabyles and the *Pieds-Noirs*. The *Pieds-Noir* took land from the Kabyles, and they haven't been forgiven."

"Jean Jacques and François meet . . . sorry, met with *Pieds-Noir* in Marseilles—also Berbers in the Kabylie in Algeria and France. There is much resentment and anti-government feeling. Strange bedfellows, you can say?"

"Yes. The enemy of my enemy is my friend."

"Exactly, I will remember that. In 1980, they have protest in Tizi Ouzo and there is still much anger against the government."

"One day in class, I noticed some writing on the board like strands of barbed wire. I knew the Berber language wasn't allowed, so I rubbed it out. I have a couple of Berber students, and if you ask me, I would probably support them."

"Yes, but civil war destroy us. Do you want it? We fight against French in 1950s to 1962. Maybe 900,000 people killed fighting for independence. You want more killing?"

Yes, I reflected. It had been ferocious, and Moussa had been born during the last few years of that war. Of course, he was right.

"I understand what you are saying. Random killings won't help anyone."

"Education, peace. We must build this country."

"Yes, as long as it is fair and equal for all." I paused, swirling the beer in my glass and watching the bubbles rise to the surface then pop. "What's my role in this?" I wasn't feeling at all comfortable, as my ignorance and naivety had allowed me to be drawn into the lion's den.

"Nothing dangerous. Like those spy films. You know, with drop-box so you can pass information. I read this in *Tinker, Tailor*."

He always surprised me. "You read the Le Carré book *Tinker, Tailor, Soldier, Spy*? I didn't know you read anything—outside of medical books."

"I want read about spies. A friend recommend, so I read book during holidays. It is like us, isn't it?"

"Yes, but remember all the intrigue. You can't trust anyone. Betrayal. So, who do you trust here? Me? Farid? Touati?"

"You, of course, Farid, Sue, and Liz. Yes. Jean Jacques? I don't know. Touati? He is only one we contact. Maybe, but we must trust him. No?"

I finished my second bottle, slugging it back. Then we both stood up.

"Not much we can do. Let's go and see what this meeting is about."

Moussa came closer to me and hugged me. "I miss you. Come back after meeting. We tell others meeting is longer. Let's go. Farid is waiting."

THREE

Before we entered the room for the briefing, a couple of young policemen searched us. They were good-looking guys, probably nineteen or twenty, but they were thorough. After patting us down, the cutest guy smiled at me. He was vaguely familiar, with bright shining eyes and clear, silky skin. As he looked directly at me, he bit his bottom lip in a genuine come-on flirtation. Then, as I walked into the room after Moussa, I felt his hand lightly caress my bum. I didn't respond, but it gave me a rush I hadn't felt for a while.

"Where have you been?" Farid looked a little petulant. "I'm here twenty minutes." Even Moussa's reassuring smile didn't relieve him of his sulkiness.

"Sorry, we were chatting. Come for a beer after. I have room upstairs."

"Maybe," said Farid, still sounding a little aggrieved.

I decided I wouldn't go, as I wanted to get back to Sue.

After a knock at the door, Captain Touati strode in. Instead of his uniform, he was wearing a light grey suit with a blue shirt and black shoes—the very look of a businessman attending a conference.

He was also a lot younger than I had first imagined, not much older than me, and he'd become a captain. In uniform, he had the authority of a military man. As a businessman, his disguise was complete. Smartly dressed, he'd slicked down his lustrous black hair, and with a light stubble of a beard, he had the fashionable appearance of a Lebanese playboy.

"Thank you for coming, and Dave, a pleasure to see you again. I hope you had a good holiday. I know this is hard, but we are making good progress. We need to get information about who is running this, and we need you as the messenger. Jean Jacques doesn't want to be seen contacting Algerians. He feels it is too dangerous. If you remember, Seamus was, umm, very open about his connections with politics, and his views and actions were dangerous." Touati paused and looked like he was having trouble knowing how to proceed. He coughed and picked up a bottle of water, twisted off the cap and poured himself a drink. "Sorry, excuse me. No, we couldn't trust him not to err, cause a disturbance or worse."

During a few moments of uncomfortable silence, the air-conditioners hummed, and I glanced out the window at the emptiness of the sky. It was embarrassing for us, as Seamus' deportation had never really been explained.

He continued, "You both teach in same school. It is natural you can meet. You both work well together, and we will protect you. Normally, of course, we wouldn't use such untrained operatives, but these times require difficult choices."

I'm not sure where that particular homily came from, but Captain Touati was doing his best, playing the good cop and trying to put us at ease. *And where did 'you both worked well together' come from?*

"Well, of course, I can't tell you everything. What you call a need-to-know basis. Basically, we need you, Dave, to be a carrier—someone who posts letters in a dead letter box and who then picks up a response—like you did before. You'll also meet Jean Jacques on an as-needed basis. It's easy. No need to worry. We will be watching. You won't be in any danger."

"If there is no danger, and no one is watching, anyone could pick up the letters. You could use Farid or Moussa." I also wondered but didn't say it: *Was I more expendable than an Algerian?*

"You will need to meet him in the open sometimes. They need to know . . . They need to . . . think Jean Jacques has a contact who funnels information to him via the French embassy. You. He will pass the information on to . . . let's call him Henri. He pronounced it the French way, stressing the last syllable, *ri.* "We will have to arrange some visits where you meet with an Embassy *function-naire.* Nothing major. I can't say any more."

Bluff, bluff, and double bluff. At last, I realized how serious this was. *Is the French government behind this or merely an element? Moussa had talked about the* Pieds-Noirs. *When Algeria became independent, they had fled to France in fear for their lives, and they must have grudges against the Algerian government.*

What do we tell Liz and Sue? The less they knew, the better, but Susan had worked here before and knew about the underlying political and social tensions. And who was this Henri?

"Oh, and one more thing, Dave." Touati motioned toward me. "We have set up Swiss bank accounts for all of you. Moussa, Farid, and you, Dave. You will find if this works out, the Algerian government is very generous."

Blood money. What was I doing? Now we are here in Algeria, we can't easily escape. My flight response kicked in, but my adrenaline junkie brain was going, "you know, this could be fun. Think of the money."

I tuned back into Captain Touati as he continued, "So, on to the details and training."

We discussed dead letter drop boxes and got a mini lecture on them.

Letterbox drops: the location must be public and secret. We should use a signal like a chalk mark to show a drop had been made. We might be passing money and/or documents. The discussion then became more open as we discussed suitable places to make the exchanges.

I could leave an envelope at Hugh's, and JJ would collect it later. *Is Hugh with British intelligence?*

Moussa mentioned a place in the palmeraie—a hole in the wall near a fig tree. I knew where, but it was rejected along with leaving a package in a café or at Al Caïd Hotel.

Then Farid suggested renting a villa in Eddis, a small village outside Bou Saâda. They would arrange for us to rent it and use it as a place to meet. It would attract less attention than in town, and the landlord was also the village chief, appointed by the FLN.

Moussa mentioned Tipaza, as it was close to the capital and lots of tourists went there. JJ could copy papers from the French embassy and drop them somewhere in the ruins very easily.

Touati reminded me of using a chalk mark to show a drop-off site had been activated.

This brainstorming session could have gone on longer but for a quiet knock on the door, and one of the policemen entered—the cute one. He spoke quietly to the captain. Touati apologized and terminated the meeting. Then the two of them left abruptly.

"What was that about?" I asked.

Of course, neither Moussa nor Farid had any idea.

Moussa shrugged and said, "Come on, let's go. I have beer upstairs in my room."

"Moussa, I'm going to call it a day and head back to the hotel to catch up with Sue. I think I need an early night."

On reaching the hotel lobby, I walked towards the hotel swing doors to look for a taxi, but someone walked up behind me, "Sir, I need check you."

I looked around, and it was Cutie. My heart pumped faster, and I had a surge of panic, but I turned to face him. His liquid brown eyes penetrated my inner being, and his whole face lit up with a childish, impish grin. He was captivating, and I couldn't stop myself from smiling back. I tried to remain calm, but my voice betrayed me. "You . . . you . . . checked me already."

He responded quietly, "Captain want speak with you. Come." He placed his hand on my arm and started to walk me to the elevators. *Is this a pick-up? He is charming.* I hesitated, not sure what to do. *Leave and get in a taxi, risk offending Captain Touati, or go with him and find out what this is about?*

Seeing me pause, the young policeman smiled broadly and leaned over, "Too much people here. I not arrest you. Room 301. Come."

We entered 301. "Where is the captain?"

"He not here."

"What do you want?" *A pretty stupid question when it was obvious what he wanted.*

"Je suis beau, non?"

"It was you at the café yesterday?"

He laughed, delighted. "Yes. My job. Follow you. Protect you. I good with disguise, no?

I looked again and had a flash of realization, "The waiter at the Al Caid Hotel?"

He smiled, his teeth white and perfect. "Yes. Now must search you."

Standing pressed against me, his urgency obvious, he passed his hands under my T-shirt. I stroked his tightly curled, cropped hair like a sensual prickly brush and closed my eyes as his gentle but skillful fingers explored my body.

"What's your name?"

He breathed, "Sami," letting it float into the air.

◆ ◆ ◆

Late in the evening, a taxi drove me through the darkening streets to the hotel. Shrugging off the ripples of guilt by repeating, *I'm a free man*, I consoled myself, knowing tomorrow would be a day without intrigue and betrayal.

I walked into our hotel room trying to look calm, but they hardly noticed. Liz immediately launched into stories of where they had been and what they had bought. And they swept me along in this light-heartedness. Tomorrow's horse riding had been confirmed, and Liz would spend the day with Moussa.

Sue and I had to be there early, so we decided to follow the old maxim: early to bed, early to rise. It gave me a sense of relief, as I didn't have to lie to answer any difficult questions.

FOUR

Our horse-riding guide, dressed in tattered jeans and a torn shirt, approached us as we stood on the sandy beach. He looked to be no more than fifteen, leading four light brown horses. They were whinnying and neighing into the cool but invigorating morning air. He shouted at us, "Me Ramli, friend Ramzi." He had a broad, friendly smile, persuading me we could trust him.

Ramzi had said he was dependable and safe, and Ramli certainly looked cheerful. However, we later learned it represented a touch of devilment and mischief rather than reliability.

The unmistakable tang of horse sweat and dung struck us as he led them closer, and he waited while we attempted to mount them. The horses were patient but snorted as we struggled to put a foot in the stirrups and swing a leg over.

Once we were safely in the saddles, Ramli led us out of the yard and toward the beach. It curved around and away from the hotel towards a ridge of hills leading to the highest, Chenoua, creating a perfect bay. The Mediterranean Sea was calm as waves lapped gently and rhythmically onto the sand. Seeing the beach peaceful and deserted, Ramli encouraged the horses into a gallop. My horse surged forward and jerked me backward at the sudden burst of energy. It was all I could do to hang on. Sue and Josephine shouted at him, and Ramli slowed the pace to a trot and then a walk.

He then led us off the beach at a gentle canter toward a wall of trees. He said one word in English, "Orange," then rode on, disappearing into a seemingly impenetrable forest. Our horses followed, and we slowed to a walk through the lush, what would normally be sweet-smelling, orange groves. But last year's oranges had been left to rot on the trees, and the aroma was over-powering, almost nauseating.

The track wove around and out into a field. After looking back and grinning, "OK?" Ramli encouraged his horse into a gallop again. Our horses, with little or no control exerted by us, followed his lead. He was showing off, letting us know he was a good rider.

Then, pushing the horses across a stream, I ducked to avoid a low-hanging branch, but it caught me. My horse rode on, my feet slipped out of the stirrups, and I was lifted into the air. Dangling and wiggling my feet, I must have looked like one of those cartoon characters suspended over a canyon. A split second later, my chin lost contact with the branch, and I plummeted into a thick, muddy pool at the side of the river. *Thwunk* and a scream of "Fuck!" before I half-choked on slime and river mud.

He had been waiting for this, probably expecting Sue or Liz to fall off so he could help them up. Looking a little disappointed, Ramli turned his horse around and dismounted. He pulled me up, trying to hide a smirk, then stood back and muttered another of his few words of English, "OK?"

I wasn't hurt, apart from my pride, and I stood up to hobble over to my horse. Ramli saw the look on my face and my dripping wet, muddy clothes. He backed away but playing the fool, I raised my fist to hit him. Then I laughed, and everyone else joined in, which eased the tension.

He helped me back up onto my horse, which had waited patiently as if this was the most ordinary thing in the world. Covered in mud and dripping wet, I followed as we turned and headed back to the beach. Then, riding our horses into the waves, we slid off into the salty, chilly sea.

Eventually we rode back to the hotel where we'd booked a room at the Tipaza Matarès. It had a magnificent, imposing entrance guarded by rounded turrets.

Once inside, Sue and I stripped off and ran into the shower, luxuriating under the hot water. We kissed, and Sue washed the mud out of my hair and the salt off our bodies. She soaped me down, and then after the shower, pushed me onto the bed and rode me.

I kept on saying, "I love you. I love you."

"I love you too," she said, but then asked, "what about Moussa?"

"What do you mean, what about Moussa?'"

"I've seen the way you both look at each other. Don't think it's not obvious. Do you have sex together?"

Sue stopped moving and looked directly at me.

"Well, do you? Liz and I were talking about it. We think you are having an affair, and rather than having it behind our backs, we want both of you to be open about it."

I must have reddened. "Yes," I said nervously. "I suppose we are. But before I met you. What do you mean you don't mind?"

"Algeria is a place to liberate you. Different rules apply here. I must admit he is really sexy. I wouldn't mind having a little bit of him myself. Liz and I thought we could have a foursome here in the hotel."

"What? Does Moussa know?"

"Yes, of course. He agreed."

I didn't know what to say. Keeping those parts of my life separate was impossible. Now they had just crashed into one another, and I didn't know how I felt. Living a life of subterfuge, I thought I had kept our affair secret. Moussa knew about Sue, but how did Sue know of my relationship with Moussa? I had been sure Liz knew nothing about Moussa and me, but now Sue suggested she did know, and they accepted it? This idea of a foursome? Maybe it would be fun, but life was getting way too complicated.

"So," she said, getting up and kissing me on the forehead, "you had better save yourself for tonight."

◆ ◆ ◆

Josephine had arranged a *méchoui* of roast lamb and invited Ramli, Ramzi, and two of her students. Liz and Moussa had arrived earlier in the evening. We all sat on the sand and listened to the waves crashing onto the beach, followed by the roar of the undercurrent sucking back the water.

The smell of roasting meat and smoke from the smoldering olive wood was irresistible. Having eaten like this before, I knew how to use my fingers. Right hand only, I had to keep reminding myself, for ripping off pieces of fatty meat, devouring it, and then tearing off more, aware of the grease on my fingers and running down my chin. I bit into a fresh, juicy tomato and a palate-cleansing raw onion.

I saw Ramli laughing and talking to the young students, and then he rolled backward, waving his arms and legs in the air like some stranded beetle. They were all chuckling and looking surreptitiously at me, so I waved at them—all good-natured. They waved back and then huddled together, whispering.

Ramli reached over, took the sheep's skull, and cracked it open. Holding it like a soup bowl, they handed it to Josephine, sitting next to them. She scooped some of the brain out and gave it to Sue on her right. It was going to come around the circle. *Please, let there be no more left by the time I get it.* The young ones watched eagerly as each one of us scooped out a portion of sheep's brain and licked our respective fingers.

However, like the others, I dipped in and scooped out the creamy brain. Then I watched as the giggling boys sliced up different delicacies and presented them on a plate. The testicles, eyes, liver, and pieces of kidney. Sue put a slice of something in her mouth, chewed it, and then carefully buried it in the sand beside Liz. I picked up some indescribable piece of offal and with a frozen smile pretended to chew. Like Sue, when no one was watching, I buried it in the sand beside me.

Finally, with fully stretched stomachs, we flopped on the sand, looked up at the beauty and infinity of the stars above us, and drank from bottles of wine. Josephine had provided Coca-Cola for her students. It was all a far cry from the arid, desert-like atmosphere of Bou Saâda.

The *méchoui* was a distraction, albeit a pleasant one, from the reality of the world we were going to re-enter. I also thought about the foursome the girls had been planning. *Why hadn't Moussa told me?* He was sitting on the beach, smiling and talking with a couple of the students. Later in the evening I noticed a young man, wearing a dark blue shirt, join the group and sit next to him. Blue-Shirt wasn't laughing or even smiling, and Moussa paid particular attention to him. Once, I saw them look across the fire at me, and then they continued talking. A few minutes later, Blue-Shirt shook hands with Moussa, got up, looked across the fire, and gave me a hurried, secret smile. *Sami.* Then he walked away, swallowed up into the darkness.

Moussa looked over at me and smiled, one of those beautiful smiles full of warmth and the joy of life. He always brought fun and joy into the group. Tonight, in the flickering firelight, he looked incredibly sexy, and I couldn't resist the intense feeling of desire welling up in me. Some people have a sexual magnetism. Was it a natural or created effect? He looked self-confident, but when you got to know him, you realized he wasn't so self-assured. He was as vulnerable as the rest of us, desirous of praise and affirmation and possessing the need to love and be loved.

He had asked if I had swooned when I saw him. Had he revealed parts of his nature to others? His insecurity, always wanting to be noticed? That time he had suddenly taken charge, changing from a charming young man into a command-and-control personality. Who was the real Moussa?

Liz giggled with Sue about something, but as they were on the opposite side of the fire, I couldn't hear them clearly. I guessed Moussa and Farid were planning how best to complete the operation Touati had outlined. I didn't want, or couldn't be bothered, to get into the details. *They don't want me there, asking questions and learning too many details. Yes, I'd agreed to help, and a successful mission meant a bonus. That's all I needed.*

We partied late and then returned to the hotel. Tired and drunk, I fell asleep almost immediately, any idea of a foursome with my best friends forgotten.

FIVE

The next day, we returned to Bou Saâda to start our second year. Farid and his FLN contacts had arranged a villa for us in a small village called Eddis. It was perfect. We had wanted to get away from town and have a place of our own so people could visit and we could have a sense of privacy.

Eddis nestled into a niche between low hills and the wide-open plain leading to Bou Saâda, about ten kilometres away. We were the only *roumis* there. *Roumi* is an old term left from the Roman conquest derived from the term used to describe Rome's conquerors, but now it means foreigners in general. It can also be disparaging when used against a non-Muslim, but it didn't bother us. We used the term ourselves as a badge of distinction. However, the village welcomed us, and our neighbours adopted and looked out for us. They were the mayor's family, and by renting his house, we paid considerably more than the going rate.

It didn't matter, as it was an excellent contrast to living in an apartment block with screaming kids, bawling parents, and an inconsiderate French teacher warming up his diesel pickup.

The first morning in the villa I woke early, drawn into the courtyard by the dawn chorus of twittering and cackles of birds calling the day into existence. It was a delightful day for late September, with the fig tree leaves reddening and the light from the early morning sun edging them in a golden halo. Hugh's comment about being here for the softness and beauty of the light floated back into my consciousness. The air was fresh and cool with a hint of wood smoke from the tandoori oven next door, which gave off a burning fragrance of newly baked *khubz*, a kind of unleavened flatbread. Soon I would be tearing off pieces and eating them, with honey dribbling down my chin.

The villa was constructed around a central courtyard with rooms on either side and a kitchen at the end. A garage, separate from the main house, allowed access to the front room for entertaining the men in true Arab fashion. Water was often a problem in Bou Saâda, but we had a storage tank in the courtyard.

The roof-top terrace gave a view of the track to the main road and north toward the distant hills. It also looked over a graveyard with a white painted Shia tomb for a Muslim holy man. The Sunni village imam told the villagers it was not Islamic, as the veneration of any dead person was strictly forbidden. However, it was tolerated as it had been there for longer than anyone could remember. Sometimes, we heard drums and a strange kind of melodic chanting coming from the cemetery in the dark of night.

We decided to have a housewarming party, so we invited expat and Algerian teachers and friends. We wanted to use it as a cover to meet Jean Jacques and get a briefing from him. We needed a quiet place where we could talk freely without the others knowing. During the evening, I managed to draw JJ away and into the private front room. Touati, Moussa, and Farid had slipped in through the garage, unnoticed by the other partygoers in the central patio. At the same time, Susan and Elizabeth entertained the guests.

Touati spoke first and directed the meeting. "Jean Jacques, what is happening?"

"It is now serious. There is money from a foreign power. Libya? I'm not sure. They want to get guns across the border and stage a coup. This group, Resist, thinks when there is armed revolt, people will join, and they will overthrow the government."

"Libya?" I couldn't stop myself from interjecting.

JJ responded quickly, "Gaddafi, he's crazy. You know this. Always trying to unite Libya with another country. Having control of Algeria will give him territory and the oil and natural gas. I've seen some agents and one of the Algerians said he recognized Libyan accents."

"The French think they can control Gaddafi?"

"I don't know. Elements in the French secret services have never forgiven Algeria for becoming independent. They want to disrupt the FLN and weaken the government, seen as powerful and corrupt. They know there are negative feelings about the wealth and control the FLN has. Remember, negotiations for oil contracts are going on now, and the French don't like the Italians—Agip especially—muscling into what the French consider their backyard."

I looked around. My mind was whirling and I had an empty feeling in the pit of my stomach.

Moussa joined in and asked, "What about Francois? What is he doing?"

I interrupted, "Who is Francois?"

"Oh no. I forget Henri is code name. Henri is in Algiers. Jean Jacques report to him."

Touati scowled at Moussa, who just shrugged. "Sorry, I forget."

I continued as I needed to know more. "So, he's working with . . . for Resist? Is he someone important?" I turned to look at Jean Jacques. "What are all these French—I mean, do you trust this Henri?"

"Yes." JJ snarled. "What a stupid—Henri is the direct contact to Resist."

I hated the way he spoke to me. Now, I understood, I was channeling my fear into hating everything about him. It was mutual. But this was my only chance to understand the situation. "Why is he involved?"

Jean Jacques regarded me with his piercing black eyes. They were cold and without a hint of pleasantry. For one brief second, Jean Jacques showed a side of himself lacking humanity. Then, with a contemptuous look, he said, "Henri's daughter has cancer, and he pays for private treatment in Switzerland. He doesn't like French hospitals and will do anything to help her."

Touati brought the meeting back under his control. "Thank you, Jean Jacques. Now we know how serious this is. I don't think Libya will have direct involvement. Those agents are probably private, for-hire soldiers, not with the backing of the Libyan government. Let's talk about practicalities. Dave, we need you to do drop-off and pickup."

The discussion continued about suitable places to exchange information, and each drop-off location was assigned a letter, A, B, etc. My mind wandered, thinking about what JJ had said about being watched. *Are the Algerians watching me? Oh, God. Why am I doing this? I had thought it would be easy. Now gun-running and smuggling across borders?* The realization that there was no way out was always at the back of my mind. I needed a completion of contract paper from the school. Only then could an exit visa be stamped in my passport. Sue and I had talked about forging one or trying to flee across the border into Tunisia, but we dismissed it as just a fanciable idea. Anyway, a part of me still wanted to see this through. *I can't desert Moussa. He's just as compromised. How will I feel later in life if I abandon my best friend?*

JJ didn't want to stay too long. We had only been away for ten minutes, but he got up to return before anybody wondered where he was. The others slipped out via the garage door, and I returned to chat with people.

It all seemed so unreal. Everyday life went on. Guests drinking wine stopped by the outdoor table, loaded with cheese, olives, fresh tomatoes, and a couscous salad. The food looked good, but I felt like my life was being played out on another planet. Then I had to return to Earth to enter a surreal, inane conversation with a teacher about one of his classes acting up.

"You know 3SA?" They were a lower-level group because they weren't taught all their subjects in French like the bilingual sections. Nodding, I scooped up some couscous.

We had nicknamed him the Black Baron. He was older and taught this class basic French and was always ready to blame the Algerians for everything. *If he doesn't like working here, why does he stay?*

"Yes? Well, AbdulAziz, the Tunisian science teacher, was teaching them. You know he's a refugee from the government there?"

"Yes."

Black Baron continued, not really wanting a response to his rhetorical question. "I heard something about him being a Marxist agitator. Anyway, he turned his back to write on the board, and one of the students threw a knife which thudded into the blackboard right beside his hand. Of course, he looked around at the class but couldn't see who had thrown it. The bastards kept quiet."

"What did he do?" I asked, trying to sound shocked, but I had heard this story before. A small knife had clattered to the floor in the version I'd heard.

"Nothing. AbdulAziz told his class not to say a word to the *proviseur* or they would all be punished. I mean, what is it coming to when you can't even turn your back on the class?"

"Of course. Isn't he a political refugee from Tunisia? He couldn't risk anything. Who told you this?"

"One of his students told me."

"Well, I've always found them to be a quiet class, pleasant and polite."

"You have no idea what is going on here. The country is fomenting. It's ready for a revolt, and yet you go on blindly teaching your English grammar and smiling sweetly at these guys as they are getting ready to cut your throat."

"Oh, come on. That's not going to happen. I like them."

He paused and looked at me in disbelief. He shook his head, drained his wine glass, and then continued. "I notice you are very friendly with Jean Jacques." I suddenly became alert. *Why is he asking me that?*

"Yes, I see him a little. We're not friends as such."

"You invited him?"

"Yes—"

He interrupted before I could continue. "I want to warn you Jean Jacques is being watched. The police—after the Seamus incident last year. What happened there?"

"Oh. I don't really know. You know as much as I do. Why do you think the police are watching him?"

"Oh, they watch us all, but Seamus was involved in something. Did you suspect Seamus of being an *agent provocateur*?"

"No. Of course not. What have you been drinking?" I said, trying to lighten up the conversation. *This is making me feel uncomfortable. I need to get away from him.*

"I think you know more than you are telling me."

I laughed a little too much. "Excuse me. I'm going to see if Susan needs any help. Talk to you later." I edged away, not wanting to prolong the conversation. I thought about reporting the conversation to Moussa or Farid. *But then, another teacher might lose his job. Maybe I shouldn't say anything. I mean, I don't like Black Baron, but he's just curious, isn't he? This is the world I am living in. I am now paranoid about every little thing said to me and looking over my shoulder all the time. Did Sami follow us down here in some new disguise? It'd be fun to see him and have him search me again.*

SIX

Every day after teaching, Sue and I left the hubbub of Bou Saâda behind and drove out into the desert to wander along dried-up riverbeds, enjoying the beauty of the desert. The air in winter was fresh and soft but, at other times, blasted you with coarse, sharp-edged grains of sand. Yet it was still exhilarating to be out battling the elements. Whatever the weather, we could always escape from the mundane. Then satiated, we returned to our little haven of tranquility in our villa set amongst the barren hills stretching behind us.

However, nature was determined to test us, and one night we suffered a raging windstorm. It crashed into our house, rattling doors and knocking on windows. One set of shutters was slamming open and shut as the wind tried to tear them off their hinges.

We suffered a restless night, listening to the cruel, howling wind tearing down on the villa. Safe in bed with a cold wind outside and snug under the covers, we listened to the storm. Sheltered and with our senses alert, we felt glad to be alive. Then a sudden calm, absolute silence and stillness, and we waited tentatively for the next bout.

Sandstorms raged over the plains in the morning, and immense red clouds blocked out the sun. Then, in the late afternoon, it became warmer and still. The sun was visible, and calm returned. But in contrast to the relative peacefulness of the weather, we didn't have electricity or gas. Our local shopkeeper told us, in broken French, about a gas-bottle shortage and delivery problem. This meant no gas bottles for heating or cooking. The storm had knocked out power lines, and even gas to fill up your car was hard to find, only a few gas stations had hand pumps to fill your tank.

The hammam was closed, but a few days before, in the late November sun, I'd bathed outside. This simplicity made the hardships in life bearable. For us, the lack of gas was a minor hardship, but for many, these shortages were far more severe.

Bedu boys stood at the side of the road with empty gas bottles as trucks with full bottles thundered past them. I doubted one would ever stop. With difficulty refilling gas bottles and without electricity, most people resorted to wood fires. In the classroom, the smell of wood smoke was pungent as students came in reeking of it. The whole family had slept around the only fire in the house. It was dispiriting and embarrassing for them not to have water to wash in. They didn't talk politics, but I felt an undercurrent of resentment towards the government in the air, like a reeking miasma.

♦ ♦ ♦

Two weeks later, after things had returned to a kind of normality, Touati suggested a quick handover like the one at Al Caïd Hotel and arranged the exchange for Eid al Adha, the holiday after the Hajj. The Islamic calendar is based on the moon phases and doesn't follow the Gregorian or Western calendar, a solar-based calendar. The date, 10 *Dhu al Hijjah,* was equivalent to October 31.

For the last four days, there had been a lot of construction with banging and sawing going on. Workers were building stalls and a ceremonial arch across the road. The local government organised a *fête* in Bou Saâda, and Touati thought a crowd would be a suitable cover for an opportunity to swap briefcases as before.

On *fête* day, I drove to the supermarket, attracted by loud gunshots. About seven or eight men were performing, slowly moving to the beat of a drum and flute. Then, without warning, they fired their muskets into the air. A loud bang and clouds of white smoke and a whiff of gunpowder haunted the air before drifting away. The crowd loved being shocked, and some bystanders had covered their ears to mute the sound. Now everyone had their eyes on the performers, trying to predict when they would fire their ancient-looking guns again.

I felt a little tap on my shoulder and turned to see Jean Jacques. He smiled, merely a pretense, but at least he was trying.

I'd never liked him, and it was obvious the feeling was mutual; but we had to play our parts, so I looked pleased and surprised to see him. This time, I had a bulky white envelope in my briefcase.

Jean Jacques had this supercilious look of disdain for everyone around him. He had straight black hair and had now grown a beard, making him look even more sinister. Yet JJ was a double agent, working, like me, for money. I had asked why we should rely on him, and Moussa told me JJ wanted to buy an apartment in Paris. Moussa also hinted at some dark secrets from his past, linked to Beau and his student days. It seemed JJ was conflicted and desperate for money in any way he could get it. *Did that make him untrustworthy?*

"Hello, Dave. The spectacle is good, is it not?"

Another explosion of gunfire and white clouds of smoke drifted into the sky. When all eyes were on the gunmen at the very second of the blast, we swapped cases.

"I'm going to get a coffee. Do you want one?"

"No, thanks," I replied. "I'm going to watch a little and see what happens."

"More gunfire, I expect. It is too loud for me. See you at school next week. *Au revoir*."

He moved away, gently working his way through the crowd, and then disappeared. I doubted anyone could even have seen what had occurred. The sun beating down on me made me sweat and feel unexpectedly weak. My legs, as heavy as lead, refused to move. I looked around and panicked, feeling trapped. *Who are all these people?*

Just before collapsing, Mustafa, a student of mine, grabbed me. "Teacher, are you OK? You are red. Come. We get drink."

"Oh, yes—hot," I could hardly stand, which was probably a reaction from the stress of waiting, and the release from the handover. I must have looked weird, and yet Mustafa smiled at me.

"Sit down this café. It is too, too hot. You're not used. You not like we Arabs. We can live in hot."

He put his arm around me as we staggered towards a café table.

"Remember, I Moussa cousin. He said me look for you and help you."

"Of course, you are all related." That sounded a little sarcastic, and I immediately regretted it. "I'm sorry."

"It OK, teacher." I think it was an automatic response, as I'm not sure he understood. He'd never been one of my better students, but he was respectful and polite. He helped me sit down and ordered glasses of mint tea and two bottles of water.

The emotion of those last few seconds had exhausted me, leaving me overheated and drained.

Gulping down the water and then sipping the hot, sweet mint tea revived me. Mustafa ordered *beignets*: deep-fried puffy circles of dough sprinkled with sugar. Eaten hot, they were filling and a treat. Then a plate of *makrouts*: fried semolina with a trace of dates. They were crispy on the outside and soft inside. When we had finished eating all this sugar, Mustafa asked me if I felt better.

"Yes, thank you. Much better. Thank you."

"Teacher, I take you my house. You can rest. Later, will be dancing here. You must see tonight."

"No, thank you. I'm going to drive back to my villa where my wife," I called her my wife for convenience to avoid any questions about our status, "will be waiting for me."

"Don't worry, teacher. She with Moussa and other one. I do not remember she name. They wait at the house of my father. Moussa said me find you. Farid, he also there. He my brother."

◆ ◆ ◆

We ate dinner together, sitting on the floor. His mother had prepared a large platter of couscous, a couple of roast chickens and a tagine of potatoes, chickpeas, and carrots in a thick tomato-based sauce with lemon, cilantro, and dried apricots, giving it a sweet, musky flavour. We used bread direct from the tandoori oven to tear off the meat and dip in the sauce. As always, there was a lot of food, but what we left was for the women and children, who had to wait in the kitchen. The men chatted in Algerian Arabic with some French expressions mixed in. I could understand odd words but had no real idea of the direction of the conversation. It didn't matter, as it was the act of shared eating that mattered.

Later, when cooler, I went with Mustafa and Farid to see the musicians and dancers. The women were advised not to go. As usual, it would be an all-male spectacle, and Moussa kindly offered to stay and entertain them.

There was a small stage with a cleared space on the ground in front of the spectators. It was amazing to see so many men in one place all at the same time. On the stage, a young Algerian man sang while two others strummed their *ouds*. Four male performers danced with hands raised and twisted their bodies with slow, undulating hip movements. The spectators joined in, rhythmically clapping and supporting the dancers.

Mustafa and Farid pushed through the crowd until we had an unobstructed view among the privileged at the front. Next to us stood a young policeman wearing an expensive blue shirt and an unzipped leather jacket. He stood a little apart from everyone else with a confident air and the aura of someone significant: a military police-type. There was a threatening ambience about him with a look of unflinching authority. Neither Farid nor Mustafa knew him, but they didn't like me asking. The leather jacket made him stand out from the standard police uniforms. He resembled a motorbike cop from California. If it had been daytime, he would have been wearing mirrored sunglasses. However, I knew it wasn't my friend from Algiers. Where was Sami? Was he undercover again and following us? I couldn't see him and forgot about it, as we watched the performance.

A couple of hundred people were listening and appreciating the free concert. Everyone swayed in time with the music, but it suddenly changed from a gentle wave into a whole mass of humanity surging forward. Almost simultaneously, the regular police waved their truncheons and moved against them. Our policeman stood and watched. *Who is he watching: us, the dancing, or the crowd?*

After a while, we decided to leave, but I noticed Farid gave a slight nod to the policeman. *So, they did know him. One of the same policemen who had searched us at the hotel? Do they alternate?*

We went back to Farid and Mustafa's place, but Liz and Sue were with Moussa somewhere else in the house. They showed me their collection of Beatles, Rolling Stones, and Tom Jones vinyl records. Both Farid and Mustafa were young and good-looking with an air of innocence that made them attractive, and I enjoyed their exuberance and the music.

Farid put on the Rolling Stones' "I Can't Get No Satisfaction," but I mused about what they understood. *Was playing the song a subliminal message, or was that how they felt as young men in a country where meeting girls was so complicated?*

He asked me a little hesitantly, "Do you like Tom Jones?"

"Yeah, of course."

"We've got 'Green, Green Grass of Home.'"

"OK, put it on."

The music flooded the room, seeming to strike a chord with them, with the reference to family particularly relevant.

They played it three times until I persuaded them to put on Elton John's "Yellow Brick Road." It was like a musical trip down memory lane—all the sixties and early seventies records.

Farid opened a bottle of Cuvée du Président. The thick red wine always had the effect of energizing me and then sending me into a deep sleep.

◆ ◆ ◆

The next day, Sue told me they had wanted me out of the house so they could have fun with Moussa. She relished telling me, and I must admit to feeling angry I'd been excluded and sent off with the younger ones. Even so, the music session had been fun.

"Whose idea was it?" I asked.

"Mine. I have always wanted Moussa. He's so sexy and sweet."

"Sweet? What do you mean? There you are, doing it, and Liz as well, and I'm sent out to watch some Arabs dancing."

"We had a threesome. I loved it."

"So, the sex was good. Don't you feel you betrayed me?"

"Are you jealous?"

"Yes. No. Fuck! You can do what you want with Moussa, but . . ." *What else can I say? Start a furious argument and end up on the losing side? I am hardly blameless. Sami's haunting smile floated into my consciousness.*

"We are still a couple, and I do love you, sweets. But I needed something different." Sue said this with an air of knowing what she wanted. We weren't married, so I had to swallow any feelings of jealousy.

"I'm surprised at Liz. I thought she was so middle-class and suppressed. She certainly has come out of her shell."

"That's what being here does for you. It gives you license to be different and enjoy the pleasures of life." Sue retorted.

SEVEN

Another week of teaching and the weekend was upon us. Moussa had arranged to see us at the villa and sent word via Mustafa that he and Farid were coming to visit this weekend. We didn't have a phone, so it wasn't easy to contact people quickly. Looking back on it, I think I preferred it. It was less stressful. Then letters could take days to reach their destination, so people passed on messages through friends who had phones. Nowadays, we feel we have to respond immediately to every text message or email we get, and we worry why the person we've sent it to hasn't responded. I miss things about Algeria, including living simply and doing without what are thought of as basic essentials. We lived on the edge at times, but we knew we were alive. Until . . .

Moussa arrived with Farid and Captain Touati in mufti, and Liz and Sue joined us in the front room.

"This coming holiday, we want you to travel south to Tamanrasset. You will be a group of tourists visiting the sites and travelling around. It's a beautiful area and very popular, lots of Western tourists. We need eyes on the ground. Jean Jacques will also be in the area with some others. Henri also." He pointed at a map produced for airline pilots. We had bought the same maps in London. "You are going to be observing."

"How will we contact you?" Sue asked.

"We have two-way radios so you can call in your reports. Don't worry. We will give you basic training. It's not dangerous, as we will be there. As tourists, you can mix in easily. You won't be noticed."

Moussa interrupted, "We will go camping. I have four-wheel drive pickup with camping things. Touati has bought you Land Rover. We camp some days and visit hotel in Ghardaïa and Tam."

"In Ghardaïa, yes. In Tam, you will be camping," interrupted Touati, "the same as the French. Later, you can drive around the Hoggar Mountains and do as you like. Of course, we will be paying for your trip down, but I think you like camping."

"What," Sue asked a little warily, "will they be doing down there?"

"Oh, do not worry," he said a little offhandedly. "We want you to observe. Take photos, drive around. This is a holiday for you. We need you to go down there and let us know what you see."

It all sounded so simple. Drive down, do some camping, watch people, take photos, move on. Moussa told us we, or more precisely he, didn't have a choice and begged us to help him. It was also a chance to have a holiday together. "Don't worry. We will enjoy. You like camping, and I have never go to South before."

◆ ◆ ◆

Now, looking back, I know Moussa didn't tell us everything. But I had no way of knowing, and when I asked Farid all these years later, he clammed up and said he would tell me later. Then I remembered events had spiraled out of his control, and we were all forced to act together without any help from Touati and his cronies.

♦ ♦ ♦

One night, about a week later, I had to meet JJ in the roast chicken café frequented by the youth of Bou Saâda. I went with Sue to have a meal and put my papers and a letter on the table. JJ would pass by and "accidentally" knock them to the floor, then pick them up for me, making the switch as he did so.

However, as he knocked them off the table, a waiter stooped to pick them up. They both reached down at the same time and banged heads.

Standing up, the waiter had the papers in his hand, and he put them back on my table. I didn't know if this had been planned or if it was a coincidence.

Jean Jacques stood up, rubbing his head. "Ah, *bonsoir* . . . May I join you?"

"Yes," I said, trying to ascertain if the waiter had taken the envelope I had to pass on to JJ. If he did, it meant they knew about us.

The resulting stress combined with the heat of the café, the overpowering smell of roast chicken and grease, and the empty plates piled with half-eaten chicken and mounds of rice made me want to vomit. I got up and rushed to the toilet to throw up. The sounds of my retching must have echoed around the café.

As I staggered back into the dining area, everyone stared at me: A sorrowful sight with my hair plastered over my forehead, hot, and a sweaty green under the harsh lights.

Both Sue and JJ got up, quickly picked up the papers, and helped me out of the café, apologizing to all in the restaurant.

My sickness allowed him to swap the papers while helping me out into the fresh air. He feigned concern, but I had never really trusted anything about him. After helping me into the backseat of my car, he asked Sue if she could drive me home. She nodded, and JJ disappeared into the darkness.

♦ ♦ ♦

At times, when walking around town, going to the supermarket, or driving up to school, I had the feeling someone was following me. *Paranoia? Even if I'm being followed, maybe it doesn't mean anything. Or perhaps it's Sami, keeping an eye on me. Wouldn't he contact me?*

The next drop, I was told not to meet JJ. We weren't to be seen together, as it was getting too obvious. They probably wanted to avoid a scene like the chicken restaurant debacle or CRD, as my friends called it.

"Don't do another CRD," Liz said to guffaws of laughter at my expense.

"It's dangerous," Sue joined in, and I had to laugh. "Maybe the waiter was part of the rebel group and had been watching JJ, wanting him to find the double-agent chicken."

I laughed, knowing it would lead to more jokes, as they wouldn't take it seriously.

"Yes, and maybe the double-agent chicken had a secret message stuffed up its arse, waiting for you to pull it out." Liz said, almost choking with laughter as the others joined in making double-agent chicken jokes and gagging noises as they pretended to throw up.

A few glasses of wine and my so-called friends could become remarkably silly.

EIGHT

An Algerian film director arrived to make a TV film series called *Barbed Wire* about the Algerian revolutionary war against the French army. They needed extras, but most French teachers declined to participate, as they felt it would be biased against the French. Of course, it was a government propaganda film paid for by the FLN, but for me it was an opportunity to be in a movie. They had to film at night so that it wouldn't disrupt people's work during the day. I was an extra, but who would know that back in the UK? I could embellish the role I had to play and add it to my resume. I also felt I deserved a chance to do exciting things away from this spy game.

However, Captain Touati found out about it and was immensely pleased, according to Moussa. He suggested a rendezvous with Jean Jacques one night during the filming. *I can't even join a film without it being tied to espionage.*

A barber cut my long, beautiful mess of hair short and shaved my beard. Then shorn, I became a young recruit wearing a French soldier's uniform. It was all so real: the dust dancing in the firelight, the soldiers resting, talking, and dragging on the butts of cigarettes, military jeeps and weapons stacked in front of tents.

I had been transformed from a high school English teacher to a real-life soldier, carrying a rifle and waiting to go to battle. But I felt uneasy. *I'm a pacifist, for Christ's sake. What am I doing enjoying this make-believe? How to reconcile this? Ah yes, it isn't to show the glory of war. It will show the brutality and inhumane nature of fighting and killing, and I can help portray the message.* The devil in my head answered with a practical slant. *Stop fooling yourself. You're just an extra wanting to act in a film.*

The first night, there was no plan to meet JJ. I saw a French *coopérant* who worked in one of the schools but ignored him.

Mustafa appeared and ran over to me. "Teacher, good I see you. You are soldier. You look strong in uniform. Come. Let's go to fire. I am Algeria resist fighter."

"Resistance fighter." I couldn't help correcting him.

"Oh. Thank you, teacher. You are two: soldier and teacher. Good."

Was that sarcasm? I laughed. "I'm sorry. I will try not to be a teacher."

"But you are good teacher and must I learn. Correct me all time."

I didn't want to dampen his enthusiasm, so I didn't comment and asked instead, "Is Moussa here, or Farid?"

"No, not tonight. Farid maybe tomorrow night. He sleeping now."

We walked over to the fire burning in a large oil barrel. I thought about the irony of being a French soldier in the army of occupation, talking with one of my seventeen-year-old students. They, in a different life, would be intent on killing me. In the same way, as a young French recruit, I would be trying to kill him. The magic of the cinema! But it's not so magic, as it's all shot in the dark and the cold with a lot of time waiting.

"*Allez. En place. En place.*" The call to action. I had to leave and follow directions. Mustafa disappeared to fight the French army.

We were raiding a village to look for terrorists. It was late at night, and we had to smash down doors and take the terrified villagers—men, women, and children—for interrogation. This take was of the French soldiers entering the village.

I charged down a street of stone-built Arab houses with the other soldiers, busted open a door by kicking it with my foot, and then threw in a hand grenade. I flung myself against a wall, waited for the blast, leaped in, and dragged out an older man with a white beard. He resisted, and I threw him against the wall smashing my rifle butt into his face. Facing the camera, blood spurted out of his mouth.

"Arrêtez."

I looked at him and spoke a little of my Algerian Arabic to put him at ease.

"Le bes?" (Are you all right?)

"Aiwa. Le bes." (Yes, all right.)

"Je suis Anglais. C'est un film seulement." (I am English. It's only a film.)

"Oui," he replied, sad and tired.

They wanted to repeat the action. We shook hands and went back to our places.

This time, the second shoot, I charged down a street of stone-built Arab houses, jumped up to kick open the door, and fell flat on my back.

"Arrêtez."

A few guffaws as the onlookers enjoyed the scene of me kicking the door and then ending up on the ground—the brutal French soldier on his back with his legs in the air. We repeated the action.

After the take, while waiting in the dark and cold for lights and action, the soldiers smoked and talked to pass the time as technicians changed the lights, and the same scene was filmed again.

With cold feet, my mind fixated on eating, warmth, and bed, but we didn't finish until 2 a.m.

Another day, at Oul Tam—a small, almost nonexistent mountain hamlet—we rode in half-tracks to destroy the mud houses. For two minutes on film, we worked for seven hours. The Army Jeep ran out of gas, so they had to siphon some from a car. It then had to be jump-started because it had a flat battery.

It all took so long in the cold mountain air. We stood around fires waiting, warming our chilled fingers and icy feet in army boots. The Arab women wearing thin, cotton-print dresses were blue with the cold.

They wanted my Western face for camera shots, and I still hadn't contacted JJ, but Mustafa kept on coming up to me and saying, "Tonight."

The feeling of being in uniform with a real gun gave me flashes of what it must have been like. Most of the extras, the French soldiers, were Algerian army recruits. They'd burst into Arabic the moment the filming stopped, shattering the illusion. No one talked to me, perhaps because they thought I was French. They were farm boys, totally different from the students I taught at school who were more sophisticated, the sons and daughters of *commerçants*: shopkeepers, government employees, accountants.

The next night, we filmed the French army in a rout escaping from an ambush. After a few takes, we huddled around a fire in an old oil drum, gaining what little warmth we could. My compatriot soldiers ignored me, talking loudly and bursting into laughter.

One soldier, who must have been only seventeen or eighteen years old, was wearing a helmet that drowned the top of his face in shadow. While talking, he expressed himself with his hands and then returned one to his crotch, fondling himself.

This youth looked at me, took off his helmet, raised his head a little, and looked directly at me. His face, lit by the flames, appeared full of life and desire. His eyes motioned out of the circle of darkness and toward the forest. But I shook my head. He replied cheekily with a slight wiggling of his head and rolling of his eyes. I smiled back.

Another night, we had filmed the local population dropping in to provide information. We were in a forest, standing around a blazing fire, trying to keep warm. The smell of burning wood and smoke was almost overpowering. I had to gulp down water to stop myself from choking, but it didn't seem to affect the Algerian farmhands. Closing my eyes, I listened to a foreign army talking.

Waiting for the next take, I watched the soldiers' faces lit by the flickering flames of the fir branches sending up showers of sparks. They illuminated the giant, threatening trees that encircled us.

Mustafa appeared and beckoned to me. I walked away from the warmth toward the forest, which enveloped me with cold fir branches, catching at my clothes and swishing in my face. Just ahead of me, I could make out a faint flickering torchlight. *Was this a trap?* A branch cracked, my heart thumped, and I involuntarily breathed in sharply.

"Mustafa?" I called quietly.

"*Ici.*" Jean Jacques said. For once, I was relieved to hear his voice. "We need to talk. We don't have time. Just shut up, listen, and don't ask questions."

The relief of hearing his voice quickly changed to irritation and anger, but I pushed it back down and strained to listen to what he was saying. "What do you know about what's going on?"

"Nothing much."

"They are planning a coup. I've told you this already. A full-scale takeover of the country. They will provide weapons, and the *putain de merde* think the *Pieds-Noirs* will join them. Then the Berbers and others will overthrow the government."

"Right." I nodded. But this was all too dramatic and crazy to be believable. "When?"

"When what?" he snapped, his voice full of contempt. "When? Listen. And shut the fuck up."

I stayed silent, feeling like a small cog caught up in intrigue more significant than I could ever understand. *I am being used, but loyalty to my friends is more important. I love Moussa and Sue; without them, I can't contemplate a future.* JJ interrupted my rambling thoughts.

"I'm going to get information about the weapons coming up from Mali and across the border. You don't need to know who from, but it is essential this is handed over to Touati. Understand?"

"I . . . I . . . Yes. I . . . I . . . under . . . stand." I stuttered, hating his condescension toward me.

"Here." He thrust a small envelope into my hands. Everything about him was aggressive, and he continued speaking dismissively. "Now go."

I turned and blindly pushed through the uncaring trees. JJ still unnerved me, and I tried hard not to burst into tears. Staggering through the forest with the branches slapping and scratching me like devils clawing at my face, I stopped to piss, fumbling with the buttons before I peed all over myself. Angry for showing him my fear, I also hated him for talking to me like that. "What a fucking bastard!" I mouthed to the silent trees, witnesses to my humiliation. *What was up with him? Is he just as conflicted and messed up by all this? If so, it makes him more human, but I still hate him.* At least JJ was someone concrete to discharge my fear and anger onto.

Mustafa must have heard me trampling through the forest. I detected a low whistle and returned the call. I was still shaking when he found me a few minutes later.

"It's OK. I listen what he say. He afraid. You good man. Don't worry. We help you."

"Mustafa, you were there?"

"Yes. I must to look after you. I brother Farid."

I couldn't help myself. The teacher in me came out to correct him, and I said very carefully, "No Mustafa. Listen. I am Farid's brother."

I heard the alarm and confusion in his voice. Then he said very carefully, "No, teacher. You wrong. I am Farid's brother." He paused for a second and then burst out laughing.

I truly enjoyed teaching these guys. They loved joking around, and they had a great sense of humour. I had set myself up for that one, and I knew that story would make the rounds of the school tomorrow.

Mustafa guided me to the edge of the forest and then disappeared into the darkness.

◆ ◆ ◆

Over the next few days, I slowly recovered, vowing not to let JJ unnerve or upset me.

What also helped was Moussa telling me that a large sum of money had been put into our Swiss bank accounts. He laughed. "We have too much money."

We spent a lot of time together talking about what we would do with all this money. "Together we buy restaurant in Nice and serve couscous. I finish study and get job as doctor. Oh, this city is so beautiful. There, I have many cousin."

We had such beautiful dreams. I weep now to think of what might have been.

NINE

The next drop was arranged for Tipaza. Jean Jacques went to Algeria to pick up documents from the embassy, photograph them in his hotel room, and then pass on the film. Captain Touati had given detailed instructions on where to do the drop, and he was anxious to get the information as soon as possible. As always, I had to pick up the "mail" and replace it with an envelope containing money and documents.

For me, a trip to Tipaza was always relaxing and pleasant, and Sue wanted to come too. We could visit our friends in Hadjout and stay with them. It also meant we had good cover to make it look like a typical visit.

As we were being paid so well, we treated Josephine and Cameron to a meal in Hadjout. The place had been plastered with red mud for the "authentic" look, with a few old farming implements hung on the walls adding to the rustic charm. Low walls divided the tables, making them look like cattle stalls. It looked a little over-designed with lamps on the tables, but we had nothing like this in Bou Saâda.

The food was good: fresh fried fish served with piping hot fries and a salad of lettuce, tomatoes, olives, and raw onions. All cooked simply, so no sauce dulled the flavour of the fish. We

163

drank two bottles of Algerian rosé wine, *Pelure d'oignon*, which means onion skin in English. Not too grand a name for a wine, but there was no taste of onion in the wine we drank! A bit of a wine freak, Cameron held up a glass to show the transparency and beautiful light colour of the rosé.

After a couple of bottles, we were merry enough to sing "The Blaydon Races" and other Geordie folk songs. Sue drove us home, but being American, she couldn't join in. However, the three of us belted out the words with more gusto than musical aptitude.

The next day was drop-off day. I didn't tell my friends what I had to do, so we arranged to meet them at the beach after our pilgrimage to the Roman ruins. We had the ruins to ourselves in the early light of the morning. The Algerians and tourists usually came after Friday midday prayer to picnic on the rocks.

I had to find twin Roman amphorae full of tall prickly pear cactuses, leave the documents in the right-hand one, and draw a small chalk line on the second. Sue posed for a photograph, and while posing she dropped the letter and marked the opposite gigantic plant pot. Safely done, we left and walked casually down the old Roman colonnade street to admire the Mediterranean Sea, gently slapping against the stonework of the ancient port.

A few tourists walked past, taking photos and ambling down to the sea. Then JJ arrived, picked up the envelope, dropped something, and moved quickly away. There was nobody around. We lingered under the shade of an olive tree with a gnarled, twisted trunk, then casually strolled over to retrieve the package. I quickly stuffed it into my bag.

Now with an envelope containing what I guessed to be a roll of film, and as in pass-the-parcel, I wanted to be rid of it ASAP. Still, to keep up the pretense, we meandered to the ruined amphitheater, took a few photos like tourists, and then just as casually wandered to the café.

The owner welcomed us and asked if I would like to see the special for today. Following him into the kitchen enclosed at the back, I passed him the envelope as arranged, and ordered the meat stew that smelled good, but I wasn't sure that was what I wanted on such a hot day.

Sue played lookout and sat at the nearest table to the exit, looking casual but observing to see if anything was out of place.

As I sat down at the table with Sue. The owner walked over to the only customer: an Algerian youth wearing jeans, a black leather jacket, sunglasses, curly black hair, spotted face, and the disdainful sneer of a thug. He said a few words to him, presented the bill, and very discreetly handed him the envelope.

Thug Boy dismissively threw some money on the table and, putting on his helmet, swept past us. He jumped on his bike and twisted the throttle, which created clouds of blue smoke and loud cries of anguish from the engine. He gunned the engine again and then raced away in a cloud of choking smoke and dust: quite a stunning exit.

Was he mad he'd waited for a few minutes or just showing disdain for expats? The motto "Hide in plain sight" certainly wasn't his. He'd roared off, leaving a cloud of dust and eventually, peace to resettle softly in the street.

It had all happened so quickly. But now, I didn't feel like staying. We left by the back streets, looking carefully all the time to see if we were being followed. Sue drove us to the hotel at Tipaza Materès, and we strolled in to meet our friends on the beach.

TEN

Before the December holidays, Touati had arranged for me to sell my Renault 16 hatchback and buy a sand-coloured Land Rover Safari. My Renault had been on many adventures, but it was unsuitable for desert driving. Bruce, as Sue insisted on calling our desert explorer, was only four years old. Touati wanted us to have him so we could get off-road, and he reckoned a British-made vehicle would fit our image.

Moussa had found or been supplied with an older Toyota Jeep, the classic Land Cruiser 40 series: a two-door, short-wheelbase pickup with a canvas cover on the back to store our supplies, camping gear, and anything else we could throw in. Moussa, less romantic about cars, refused to name his vehicle, calling it a truck. Liz, happy to be with him, rode shotgun, and at times also drove.

Earlier in the day, we had stopped in a small town, Berriane, to fill up with gas along with two spare 20-litre jerrycans and four 20-litre containers of water. Moussa, in his Toyota four-wheel-drive truck, packed them in the back. We then took a walk around the town and ended up in the market.

It looked peaceful. A man sprawled on the sand, trickling the red grains through his fingers and two women sat over their wares, a few bracelets and odd trinkets, but no one was buying. A few

166

people ran past us, and then we noticed a mass of men huddled around a door. Some pushed to get in, and others struggled out, clutching hard-won cans of tomato paste, condensed milk, and sugar. The delivery truck from the North had arrived.

Standing at the top of a slight rise, I noticed a figure wearing a hooded cloak observing the crowd. I assumed it was a man, but he looked strangely sinister, especially with the hood hiding his face. However, we were in a hurry, so dismissing the image, I ran to catch up with my friends. The marketplace was full of men, and both Sue and Liz mentioned they felt uncomfortable, with a feeling that we didn't belong.

We heard shouting and watched as a mass of men swarmed the butcher's shop—a wooden shack, with the severed heads of a goat and a cow hanging on hooks outside. Blood dripped to the ground, and flies swarmed over pools of the slowly congealing mess. The buzzing of the hundreds of flies was incredible, but they were ignored by the men as they pushed and shouted to get fresh meat. A hunk of gore was passed over the heads of the crowd to an older man in an army greatcoat. He stuffed it into an inside pocket of his coat and shuffled away while a donkey waited patiently.

Liz stated quite emphatically, "Into the 'Heart of Darkness.' From now on, I'm going to be a vegetarian."

Sue agreed, sickened by the lumps of meat, the flies, and the blood dripping from the hacked-off heads with their eyes staring dully at you. We renamed the settlement as Hacked off Heads.

◆ ◆ ◆

A routine had developed over the last few nights. On leaving the main road and venturing into the desert wasteland, we looked for a suitable camping spot far enough away from the road to dissipate the rumble of the trucks thundering down the road.

Sitting around a campfire and chatting, we looked up and marvelled at the night sky. The Milky Way was so clear, revealing to us a breathtaking scattering of glittering white stardust, millions of light-years away. We recognized the Big Dipper, plotted the North Star, and could see Orion striding across the heavens.

Being on holiday and visiting the South for the first time, we took a detour to Ghardaïa, a town famed for being unique in Algeria. I didn't see it the last time with Steve. *Poor guy, he'd been so eaten up with jealousy over Sue. Not worth it.*

The M'zabites had built the town and surrounding date palm trees. They are known to be more hardworking and industrious than the average Algerian. Moussa was a fount of knowledge about them but was wary of what he considered the sect's hardline on women and Islam.

He told us they had not been allowed to settle in the north of Algeria and eventually found this deserted rocky area to build their farms. Yet, he admitted he was impressed by their ability to create a beautiful, fertile area using a system of irrigation canals.

The town of Ghardaïa stands on a hill and looks fortified, which was one of its functions during periods of unrest. The houses spread up the slopes to form a pyramid with the prominent minaret of the mosque centred at the summit. It is a shock after having driven across the endless, monotonous desert to discover this architectural gem.

Ghardaïa is the main town with smaller settlements, like satellites, radiating out from it. These towns are populated mainly by the M'zabites: the original Berber inhabitants of North Africa. Farid mentioned that due to inbreeding, they have various genetic similarities. One of these is poor eyesight, resulting in many of the men wearing jam-jar-like glasses. He told us the men look and dress very similarly but are known for their hard work as traders and businessmen.

The *Guide Bleu* stated that many famous architects had made a "pilgrimage" to Ghardaïa to study it. We admired the square buildings painted in soft pastel colours. Le Corbusier, a modernist

French architect considered one of the most influential architects of the 20th century, visited the then French colony of Algeria in the 1930s. The Moorish style fascinated him, and he wrote about the simplicity of form and the recurring images of the cube-shaped houses of colour.

We found a hotel and then walked up the streets leading to the central market below the mosque. Farid wanted us to observe the people, but who? There were a lot of visitors. Like a tourist, I took photos of buildings and people, but carefully as I didn't want to upset the older, more traditional men. Quite a few of our colleagues were travelling south, which provided excellent cover for us as we didn't stand out.

It was a provisioning stop as well, so we stocked up for the next few days, buying fresh fruit and vegetables from the men seated on the ground. I noticed an older man in a suit with a pretty, younger woman holding on to his arm, and I wondered if she was his daughter. I watched him buying fruit from a seller and passing it to a young, well-dressed man—the chauffeur? They stood out, as most people dressed casually in jeans and T-shirts, unlike the older men in traditional cloaks and turbans.

The narrow streets leading off from the market cast dark shadows and attracted by the promised shade, Sue and I left the market square to explore the city, away from the buzz of people. It was quieter, but as men walked past, we had to squeeze ourselves against the walls. It was confusing and maze-like, with winding streets and sharp corners.

A door opened, and a man wearing a long cotton *djebella*, thick glasses, and a bushy black beard glared at us angrily. He waved his arm in the direction we had come, shouting in Arabic, "Emshee." (Go.)

Feeling unwelcome, we turned to follow the winding streets, leading back to the noise and bustle of the market, but at the first corner, I turned and glanced back, and a shadow flitted behind the corner of a building. Was it my paranoia again? Are we being followed?

Beni Isguen, a "must-see," is a smaller walled town, closed to nonbelievers after sunset, but Moussa and Farid didn't want to go.

"I'm not comfortable," Moussa explained, "being seen in the town with women. They'll ask questions."

However, Liz, Sue, and I decided we didn't want to miss something described as unique. Our obligatory guide was friendly but strict about where we could go and told us photography was forbidden. The men ride donkeys, as no cars are allowed in this walled town with narrow, winding streets. At night, the city closed its heavy wooden door and shut itself off from the outside world. It was a trip into a long-ago past.

We returned to our hotel to enjoy the treat of sleeping in a bed again. Because none of us were married, Moussa had booked three rooms. We enjoyed the luxury, but it was easy to see why camping was a better choice. We were free to do as we liked without worrying about how we would be perceived by others. Ghardaïa was merely a refreshment stop to clean up, provision, sightsee, then get back on the road.

The journey south was pleasant enough on a newly tarmacked road. But after seventy kilometres, we passed construction teams levelling and packing the new highway. Then we hit the corrugated track. Driving on this *piste* was similar to driving for hours over a washboard. As vehicles race over the ground, the vibrations create ridges and dips, which become hardened and form a rigid, furrowed surface. Some people claim driving at a certain speed allows you to float over the ruts. One "expert" suggested eighty kilometres per hour, but even he admitted it could damage the car. The *piste* shook and jolted every joint, stressing the shock absorbers, but going slower was even worse as it increased the harsh judders after each corrugation.

I increased speed, but as we were following Moussa, his truck stirred up clouds of dust that poured through our open windows. We had to close them to avoid choking, but it only increased the oppressive heat in Bruce. I slowed down to let the swirling dust settle. Then we could open the windows and speed up to get a cooling breeze, but with the windows open, bits of paper and my hat flew around the car and escaped into the wilds of the desert. I drove on, kicking up dust and stones.

One time, a truck behind us honked loudly and then sped past, covering us in clouds of sand fine enough to choke us and kicking up sharp rocks, which whirled up and smashed into the car. One hit the windshield but luckily didn't shatter it.

Passing oasis settlements of mud houses and palm trees, we were drawn onward by the shimmering mirages of lakes caused by the baking heat in the middle of the day. The farther south we went, the hotter it became. Even though this was winter, the temperature hovered around thirty-five degrees Celsius. We stopped to have a break and a lunch of sardines, tomatoes, and two-day-old bread.

I read from *The Travelers Guide to Algeria.* "A mirage is described as a refraction of light. As the colder air moves through, it is bent by the hotter air." Nobody seemed to be listening. "I suppose it's rather like those science experiments where they show light going through a prism and emerging as different rays of colour."

"Never mind the science," interrupted Sue. "The heatwaves from the sun are slowly broiling me. Let's go."

Old smashed-up vehicles littered the track, "Tam or Bust" painted on their skeletons. We passed empty hulks of Volkswagen Combis and Citroën 2CVs, blackened by fire or stripped to bare metal. We imagined them being picked over by marauding bands of Bedouin, emerging out of the desert to scavenge and pillage the broken prey left behind.

That night we left the main road and followed a track into the desert wilderness, heading to a small canyon cut into a distant mountain. It gave us a feeling of protection and helped us disappear into the vastness of the desert landscape.

Early in the cold morning air, Sue boiled water on the camping stove to make coffee, and for breakfast we ate dry toast spread with *La Vache qui rit* (The Laughing Cow), cream cheese, and bananas.

While eating, we watched the shadows of the hills creeping further away as the sun climbed in the sky. Then, warmer, the trucks packed, we continued our journey south into the Heart of Intense Brightness, as Sue now laughingly called it.

Nearing Assekrem, the dirt road wound its way past columns of rock, thrust up like standing phalluses. They created stark shadows across the plain. Erect and defiant, they dwarfed the thorn bushes and solitary trees struggling to survive in the dried-up watercourses. It was unnervingly quiet. A snake twisted and slithered across the track in front of us. Bruce motored on, lumbering over gravel and hard rock with the hot desiccating air embracing us. Affected by the heat, inhaling the fine, gritty dust, and suffering from exhaustion, we became irritable, arguing over food and rationing each gulp of water.

The landscape was awe-inspiring, but Bruce struggled up the track, slowly rising from the barren gravel plain of sun-blistered brown and black rock. The air was thinner, and he needed to be tuned, but spluttering and backfiring, we slowly curled up the winding mountain track. Our destination was the holy grail of Saharan travellers—the Assekrem hermitage nine thousand feet above sea level.

As the sun descended, the rock pillars cast long shadows from the rising moon over the gravel plain stretching away to the pinnacles of craggy, faraway mountains. They were menacing in the half-light as they slowly encased us in their deep, engulfing pools of shadow. I became aware of a tinge of fear: the feeling of being alone and isolated.

It was only seven, but it seemed so much later. We were tired, cold, and short-tempered. I wanted to sleep, but it felt ridiculously early. Sitting in Bruce, we waited in silence until we could go to bed to endure the freezing temperatures of the night.

ELEVEN

The hermitage at Assekrem was built high up in a stunning location overlooking the mountains of the Hoggar—a spectacle where you could experience the sunrise and watch it set in front of you. Here you could reflect on and contemplate man's existence on this planet.

Père Charles de Foucauld built his refuge in the early 1900s and founded a small sanctuary living with the Tuareg community. He used it as a retreat and lived the life of a hermit. Earlier in life, Foucauld had explored the deserts of North Africa and the Middle East as a cavalry officer and a Trappist monk before deciding to live a simple life as a hermit among the Tuareg. He learned the language and published a Berber dictionary and grammar. In 1916 a band of roving Bedouin attacked the hermitage and killed him. Catholics now consider him a martyr, and the Church was exploring his canonization.

Assekrem is maintained by his successors. It has become a pilgrimage for Catholics and a place to be checked off the list of achievements by explorers on the Sahara itinerary. I was keen to spend the night in the separate stone shelter—built to welcome visitors. We scrambled up the path to the "top of the world," then stood breathless on the plateau in front of the refuge. Sue had been here years before and brought a present of tea, sugar, and dates for the two hermit priests maintaining the hermitage and living a life of religious contemplation.

We stood at the edge of the moonscape before us: silent and respectful of the drama inherent in the view. About twenty fellow voyagers stood awed, sweating and out of breath, but stunned into silence by the vastness of the mountain vista. Far below, you could make out the campsite with a few scraps of colour and toy cars. I felt tiny and insignificant, like an ant soldiering away without any knowledge of the larger world around it. What did the double-dealing and affairs of countries have to do with anything?

We watched the sunset: an orange light illuminating the distant mountains in shades of brown, with deep shadows spreading and cloaking the edges of the craggy, broken, tooth-like peaks. The sun descended, leaving vapours of luminescence floating in the band between earth and sky.

As the night sky darkened to a deep purple, everything took on a ghostly murkiness. Rocks that had stood proudly on the sandy desert now seemed to float in a world inhabited by strange, weirdly magnificent beings: a religious experience. I was awed by the drama and splendor.

"Jinn in the Qur'an—evil spirits," said Farid. "They get into your head to make you follow the devil."

"Have you seen one?" I asked.

"No, but they are here."

A trace of a car's headlights flashed and disappeared as it followed the twists and turns of the track we had taken hours earlier, now a faint scar cutting across the pristine hills.

I wanted to sleep in the refuge with the Saharan elite: those who had spent the night at the hermitage, but Sue, Moussa, Farid, and Liz descended to the campsite below, leaving me to share my experience with other brave adventurers.

The building was primitive, with only the basic rudiments of comfort. But being a hermit is all about renouncing the pleasures and accoutrements of our comfortable lives.

Could I become a hermit? Escape the everyday demands of chasing money, love, and the desire to have an easy life? No, I'm still too involved in the real world. Perhaps, like Foucauld, I need to live first and then retire and exclude the world.

I stood on the edge of the world, hypnotized by the scene before me. The campers' lights below glittered in the dark, echoing the stars flickering in the sky above. The night sky appeared brilliant and vast. By experiencing the grandeur of the heavens, you had to contemplate man's puny existence on this planet and give thought to a life away from the intricacies and pettiness of the world around you.

The experience left a feeling of reverence and awe. I felt cleansed. Still, it didn't last long. Returning to the refuge, I re-entered my trivial alternate life. I had seen Jean Jacques and wondered if he would contact me, drawing me back into the world of subterfuge and danger.

A few young French, Swiss, and German travellers—not tourists—were sitting, smoking, and talking in low, hushed tones. "Travellers" consider themselves superior. They feel that only they fully experience the country by existing on meagre budgets, mixing with the people, and staying in flea-infested lodges. They felt better than tourists paying top dollar to fly in, see the "significant" sights, and then return home to share photos of their "Oh, Margery, it was so marvelous" holiday.

At first, I had both a mattress and an assigned bed to put it on, but as more people arrived, I had the choice of either the wooden bench or the mattress on the cold cement floor. I took the hard, wooden bed. Most of these travellers sat, smoked, talked, and laughed through the night. I knew their vehicles had the required "Tam or Bust" slogans emblazoned on them. They believed themselves genuine explorers but seemed so inconsequential as they focused on their own experiences. The conversations revolved around comparing Tam with Angkor Wat, the pyramids, or whichever place they could score with to impress their fellow "travellers."

Jean Jacques lounged opposite me on the bare concrete floor of the cold, stone building, joking and chatting with his compatriots. He didn't make eye contact. It was as if I didn't exist. Eventually, I rolled over and slept, remembering we had to look for gunrunners the next day. In the morning, a note in my jacket pocket had two stark, simple words: "The market."

TWELVE

We drove to Tam in the morning and walked over to the market. It had a once-a-year fair for the locals to stock up on items usually in short supply or nonexistent. The trade comes from Niger and Nigeria in the south, and for this week all the goods were exempt from the regular customs duty. The market was a special event for the locals, but it was disappointing for us, coming from the better-stocked North. We glanced at the white enamel bowls, gaudily coloured blankets and plastic bowls and buckets, with rubbish littering the ground. There was nothing "authentic" worth spending your dinars on. But watching the haggling was street theatre at its most raw and creative, with buyers demanding a lower price and sellers wheedling and shouting how it would leave his children to starve. Both participants played their parts and entertained the crowds.

I bought a kilo of oranges from a man sitting cross-legged in front of a pile spread out on a blue plastic sheet. The oranges were firm and fresh, with a tangy smell of sweetness. Unable to resist, I peeled one and handed half to Sue. We devoured the segments with sticky juice dribbling down our chins, and I leaned down and bought another kilo.

Looking across the market square, I noticed a well-dressed man in a suit with a pretty girl on his arm. We'd seen him in Ghardaïa, but as we were all on the same route visiting the towns in the south, it wasn't that remarkable. However, I wondered why he wore a suit, as it made him stand out from everyone else around him. I watched them buying provisions that the older man passed to his chauffeur carrying heavy shopping bags. Then I noticed them later as we rested in a café and drank reviving glasses of sweet mint tea, and at noon, they drove past in their green Range Rover.

Trade from Niger. You could easily smuggle weapons under cover of all this activity. I looked at Moussa. "Shouldn't we look for the weapons or the smugglers? Anyone here could be . . ."

Moussa winked at me. He was handsome in a roguish way. I touched his hand briefly, and it gave me a twinge of delight. "Dave. Wait. We not look for weapons now."

My overwhelming desire was to have him touch me, but it was useless, as he was intent on looking for the French.

"I see . . . saw Jean Jacques and Francois. Remember Henri? We must wait and watch."

"Francois—sorry, Henri—what's he doing here?"

"I not know. Jean Jacques said he would come. Farid and I will go to briefing. You can go to hotel and eat lunch."

I felt we were being followed, and it seemed as if the green Range Rover had been tailing us around Tam. Then, as we sauntered into the hotel, they drove into the parking area. The driver, smartly dressed and wearing mirrored sunglasses, jumped out and opened the side door. The older man in the business suit stepped out, then the young woman. Holding onto his arm, she walked with him into the lobby. She was wearing a short, tight, light blue skirt and a white blouse: smart and definitely not the usual kind of woman you saw around town. Her sandy blonde hair was uncovered and flowed down her back. She shook her hair out as they walked past us. They certainly were an odd couple, but nothing was unusual in Algeria. *Surely no spies would be so flamboyant.*

Farid and Moussa returned later, bursting into our room, grinning and pleased as could be. "We have information on gun smuggling and where the exchange will happen. The police have inside source. He tell them where. North and east of Tam."

"So, what are we supposed to do?" Liz was curious to know our role and to define it clearly.

"Nothing. It is over. We can go back. But Sue, you like rock art. There is one place with paintings. We can go. You will like it."

"How far?"

"Seventy or eighty kilometres off-road. Now we have Bruce and my truck, we can go."

"What about the police? What will they be doing?" Liz pressed for more details.

Farid interrupted, smiling, "They will watch for them at the checkpoints and report back. But don't worry. It is finished."

I know we all felt a sigh of relief. We could do what we liked. This expedition to see the petroglyphs was intriguing. Between twelve and six thousand years ago, the Sahara had been green and fertile. Rock paintings of the original inhabitants, and animals like crocodiles, giraffes, lions—now extinct in the area—had been discovered. Djanet was a famous site to the east and a popular tourist destination. However, this site, according to Moussa, was not so well-known. Sue was excited and very keen to go.

THIRTEEN

The next day, we left early. Moussa was leading in his pickup, and Liz, as usual, rode with him. Sue, Farid, and I were driving about ten minutes behind in Bruce. We had decided to meet at pre-arranged spots, usually gas stations, until we had left the road, just in case we were followed.

We'd been driving for about an hour on the newly tarmacked road when the green Range Rover shot past us. The driver looked straight at us and braked with the tires squealing as the car swerved from side to side. Then like a rifle shot, the driver's side front tire burst with a tremendous bang, and he lost control. The car flew off the tarmac and, in a split second, hit the ground, flew into the air and landed with a sickening crunch on the stony desert.

We stopped, shaken and terrified by the accident. I jumped out and ran into a scene from a horror movie. Smashed boxes of oranges, bars of soap, and now-meaningless belongings littered the ground. A semi-automatic rifle lay on the stones amidst the wreckage. *Police or rebels?* Farid picked it up, along with a box of shells lying next to it, and quickly rushed back to Bruce. I stood paralyzed, not knowing what to do.

The driver crawled out of the car and then sat stunned beside the vehicle. The older man had gone through the windshield and now lay lifeless, his skull smashed open. A young woman in a short, tight skirt lay on her back in front of me.

Before I could register what had happened, a group of French bikers rode up and sprang into action. One went off to a distant building to telephone for help. Another started CPR on the woman, pressing rhythmically down on her chest and breathing into her mouth. I watched helplessly as her chest rose and fell with the air forced down her throat, but the pale, doll-like woman I had seen at the hotel only yesterday evening died in front of me.

Farid ran up to me and took me by the arm, pulling me away while the bikers were busy. "We can't stay. We have to get away." I protested. "Why?"

"They had a gun," said Farid. "Let's go. The police will come."

We clambered back into Bruce, but Sue kept asking questions: "Who were they? Why did they have a gun?" Perhaps it was her way of dealing with the shock. However, we had no answers.

Farid repeated we had to leave. I revved the engine and left the bikers to deal with the accident and the horrific aftermath while we accelerated away to get to our rendezvous with Moussa.

After explaining what had happened, Moussa suggested heading back home, but Sue was adamant she wanted to see the rock art site, especially as very few people had been there.

"It's my turn to do what I want instead of being ordered around. This is our holiday now, and we may never get the chance again."

Liz agreed as it sounded intriguing, especially being in a closed, off-road area. The map had large areas marked "no access," but Farid explained that was to discourage people as there were no roads. So, we plotted a course away from the main road and then south, but we had to head west first.

We drove out of the gas station and turned onto a track into the desert, aiming to become invisible. Nobody knew where we were going, and it gave us a sense of relief. At last, we were explorers doing something for ourselves. We continued driving west and, in the early evening, headed towards a range of distant mountains looking for a place to camp.

Exhausted and shaken by the aftermath of the death we had seen up close, I nodded off, then shook my head to recover consciousness—the desire to stop overwhelming. A forlorn lone tree looked like a possible place to set up camp, as I felt it would give us some shade in the morning.

However, Moussa insisted it wasn't suitable. He felt it was too exposed and pointed out a black column of granite rising out of the desert. It looked like a giant mushroom, as the low-level desert winds had sandblasted the rock creating a stem and a cap resembling the fungus. Behind it, the low ridge of a mountain range merged with the night sky. The light was fading, and we probably had another fifteen minutes or so before a veil of darkness descended.

"Come, let's go to mountain there. More shelter than this tree."

We had been driving for eight hours, and I was desperate to stop, light a small fire, cook something, and then go to sleep.

"It will give shadow, out of sun. Protect us from wind tonight."

"OK, but not too much farther."

Moussa took the lead and put on his headlights. We followed behind, but farther back, to avoid the dust billowing up from behind him. He was moving fast, in a hurry to find a place to camp, but we must have been making quite a noise, and our arrival would have been evident to anyone in the area. I slowed down to negotiate a dry riverbed, going down at an angle and then climbing out the other side. When I reached the top, we couldn't see Moussa's truck, but dust clouds were settling closer to the mountain, so I knew where he had driven. I sped up as we were afraid of being left behind.

A rapid *rat-a-tat-tat* of automatic gunfire sounded. I braked, looked, then heard another burst of machine-gun fire followed by silence: A sickening, nerve-racking silence.

Then in the distance, we saw two vehicles driving rapidly to the north, their headlights rising and falling and cutting shining pencil lines into the sky. After a few minutes, another set of lights started heading toward us.

I pushed Bruce hard, speeding like crazy to catch up, but not paying attention as we lurched and swayed, hitting rocks and gliding over sandy patches until we weren't. Bruce bogged down in a patch of soft sand. Revving and gunning the motor only made it worse—the wheels were spinning, digging us farther into the sand. We had sunk up to the axles and were stranded.

Farid looked at me and grabbed the two-way radio, desperate to contact Moussa before he got out of range. He shouted, "Moussa, Moussa. What happened?"

"They shot Liz! They shot Liz!" Moussa was sobbing and screaming. The radio crackled, then faded.

"Hello, Moussa? Over."

Crackling and static and then, "I . . . get her . . . hospital. Tam. Over."

"We are stuck. Soft sand. How is she? Over."

"Bleeding . . . bad . . . You stay there. Check campsite . . . I go hospital."

"OK. Tomorrow. Look after Liz. Over."

". . . photos. Find evi- . . ."

Sue burst out, highly agitated, "What did he mean they shot Liz? Is she dead? What's going on? Who shot Liz? Use the radio. Call the police. Farid. Call the police!"

"I can't. We are out of range."

"Where are they?" She screamed in desperation. "Aren't they supposed to be helping us?"

"Not anymore. We are alone."

The evening light was fading while I tried to maneuver our way out. Cursing and shouting at the world did nothing to help but it relieved my inbuilt tension.

I jumped out and desperately tried to deflate the tires to create a balloon effect to help us glide over the sand. Farid dug out sand from the front tires to put sand ladders under them. Then I remembered I had a rubberized cushion that, when inflated, raised the car off the sand. Attached to the exhaust pipe, it slowly filled with the gases. But it all took time, and we knew we couldn't follow Moussa's tracks in the night.

"OK, Farid, get ready to push the sand ladders under the tires. Not too far, just a little to get the grip. Put the others under the rear tires, I'll disconnect the bag, and Bruce should settle onto the ladders and then we can drive slowly onto the harder sand."

It worked smoothly, but packing up and deflating the airbag took time, and the deep purple had now changed to an inky black.

I had a rough idea of where Liz had been shot and had placed a line of stones in the approximate direction—more of a guess than an accurate course, but I knew we could never follow his tracks in the dark.

Occasionally, we could see his lights tracing up into the night-time sky and then disappearing in the far distance. It would have been stupid and dangerous for us to try to follow him. There were a few stars but no moon. It was cold, and we were defeated. We had lost over an hour getting out of the sand.

"We'll do as he says. Let's make camp here and try to find that campsite in the morning when it gets lighter." I tried to sound sensible and calm, but my voice kept betraying me.

Sue sobbed. "Farid, how far is it to Tam?"

"Over a hundred kilometres."

FOURTEEN

We woke as the sun rose over the mountains, casting deep shadows of darkness. It was crisp and cold, and I hadn't slept well. Worry about Liz and Moussa had kept me turning and fidgeting through most of the night. We packed by throwing everything into the back of Bruce, saying we would sort it out later. In the early morning light, we followed the tracks toward the dark, now-sinister-looking towers of granite. Eventually, rounding a corner, we found an abandoned campsite.

I stopped and walked over to see what evidence we could find. Shell casings littered the campsite, and tire tracks showed the confusion. It was a mess: a camping stove, pans, and sleeping bags scattered on the sand. A blackened circle indicated where their fire had died out during the night.

Farid speculated Moussa had driven straight into the site. They must have heard him coming and lain in wait behind some rocks. It looked like they had sprayed the pickup with their machine guns and then jumped in their trucks and made off. How many people? We counted the footprints and reckoned possibly six. We couldn't find any blood on the ground, so Liz hadn't gotten out of the car. Neither had Moussa, as I couldn't find any footsteps near their tire tracks. We were lucky there hadn't been a strong wind last night. Otherwise, most of the evidence would have been blown away. *Were they the gun smugglers? Why had they shot at Moussa?*

Farid took photos and picked up some of the bullet casings as evidence, but then we argued about what to do. I suggested following their tracks for a while to see what direction they had gone. Eventually, we agreed to drive for about an hour and then head back east to the road and Tam. The tracks led away to the west, which didn't make any sense, as according to Farid the supposed gun swap was south. I drove slowly and carefully, following their tracks onto a ridge and down into a broad gravel plain. Mature trees showed the course of an underground river, their roots penetrating the ground and sucking up the precious water.

I could see they had turned south, following the line of trees. After twenty minutes or so of carefully navigating the twists and turns, we saw forbidding ridges of parallel dunes ahead of us, so I stopped in the shade of a tree. Time to eat and decide what to do. The sun was already beating down with an unbelievable intensity for December. With a map and compass, Farid and I tried to work out how far it was to Tamanrasset.

"It's my fault." Sue, on the edge of crying, "If I hadn't said . . ."

"We all agreed to go," I said, knowing how guilty she must feel. "Let's focus on what to do."

"We should go to Tam," Sue's voice broke as she pulled out the camping stove and a few pots, "and report this to the police. Then we can find Moussa and he can tell us what happened to Liz."

"We can't do anything, even if we do catch up."

"I'll take Bruce," said Farid, "and follow these tracks. Maybe just ten or fifteen minutes."

He drove off, the sound of the engine drifting into the silence. Alone in the middle of a riverbed with little water and not much food, I realized we would never make it if we had to walk. *Why had we let Farid drive away? What if he became lost?*

Sue couldn't eat, so we sat there for what seemed like ages but was probably less than half an hour until we heard a revving engine making its way toward us.

"What if it's not Farid?" Sue asked. "What if it's the rebels? They might have been watching us and waiting."

"There's not much we can do. There's nowhere to hide. They'll shoot us here like rabbits."

We strained our eyes, looking in the direction of the noise and praying it was only Farid following his tracks back.

"It's got to be Farid. We didn't hear any gunshots or anything, so he's driving back. He does seem to be going rather fast." I should have kept quiet, as it only increased Sue's anxiety.

Farid drove into the camp and jumped out. "I found the place where they stopped. Fresh tire tracks, and then they drove away, going south toward the rendezvous."

"Here, drink some coffee and eat." Sue handed Farid a cup of sweet coffee and some of the crunchy toasts with cream cheese. "Then we'll drive back to Tam. Moussa must be out of his mind. What about Liz? Is she badly wounded, do you think?"

"She must be," I said, "or Moussa would have driven back to Tam."

We continued going over and over the scenarios, repeating and confirming what we already knew, or thought we knew, and trying to make sense of it all.

"Whatever happened, it's not worth the money. When this is over, we're leaving." Sue was always strong-willed, but she was right. It wasn't worth the danger or the money. I did like aspects of Algeria, but to risk your life and those of your friends?

We repacked and drove off, following Farid's directions to intersect a set of tracks he had seen heading towards a ridge we had crossed earlier, but we were now much farther north than before.

"It's dangerous," I said, "one car in this desert is stupid. With two we could always get help if one of us broke down."

"Yes," said Farid, "but we'll be OK."

"We have enough water for probably four or five days if we ration it . . ."

We talked on as I maneuvered Bruce across the plain toward the escarpment. Eventually, we crossed the trail of a vehicle that had driven up onto the ridge. It looked like a scar slashed across the slope. I stopped. As a precaution, I lowered the pressure to twelve PSI, giving the tires a larger surface area to help Bruce climb up the sandy incline more effectively. I had a tire-pump so I could reflate them later. Then getting a head-start and engaging third gear, I took a run at the dune using the forward momentum to get us up to the crest. I stayed in undisturbed sand as it is better to drive on than in the previous track as this sand is softer, and we might have bogged down.

From the top, we had a view of a flat plain stretching before us. We knew the road went roughly in a north-south direction, so we continued going east, knowing we would eventually find tracks to lead us back to the highway and on to Tam.

Sue stated, practical as ever, "OK. Let's go, and when we get there, we'll check the hospital."

FIFTEEN

We hurtled down the highway as fast as possible and then followed the *hôpital* signs. We found her in intensive care.

It was heartbreaking. Liz, who had been so full of life, was reduced to a bandaged body plied with tubes and connected to a life support machine. No one could or would tell us much, just "wait and see."

It's strange, but I could only speak English. Seeing Liz in hospital was too emotional. Our friend was in a coma, and we felt helpless. Sue said she would stay in case Liz woke up, and the nurse ushered us out. We left, but Farid wanted to inform the police and get better care for Liz, thinking a guard should be placed by her door.

Dropping Farid off at the police station, I drove to the hotel to see if Moussa had reserved rooms for us. He hadn't, which didn't make sense, but I paid for three rooms and decided to go back to check on Liz and Sue in the hospital.

By 4 p.m., it was still hot and dry, with a blue sky and a baking sun. The streets were mostly empty. Then, driving back towards the hospital I saw Moussa walking along the street. Quickly making a U-turn, I returned to where I'd seen him, but the main road was deserted. The only way he could have gone was down a side alley next to a restaurant.

I sprinted up the narrow rubbish-strewn lane calling for Moussa. A door opened, and a man stepped out. He was massive, with dirty jeans hitched over an overhanging belly and biceps bulging out of the arms of a once white, now soiled T-shirt. His red face, blotchy skin, and an ugly scar running down one side gave him a menacing appearance. This was not someone, you messed with. He stood looking at me, his arms folded.

"*Oui?*" he barked out. He continued in broken French, worse than mine. "What you want? This no exit. What you want?"

As I didn't turn around and go back, he shouted at me in Arabic. He began by calling me a cow's arse, a motherless child. I didn't move, didn't react. Then finally, he called me a shoe—the greatest insult. Think about all the dirt and shit you walk on. It's strange how you learn the insults first. Moussa had taught me as a bit of fun.

I knew this was getting serious, but I had to ask about Moussa. The man moved closer to me. Hulk (as I silently named him) stank of stale beer, grease, and cigarette smoke. I guessed he worked as a cook in the restaurant on the main street.

I forced a smile and said politely, "*Masa Al Noor.*" (Good evening.)

Hulk merely looked at me and moved even closer. I backed up against the opposite wall. He stuck his face close to mine. Inhaling his stale sweat and foul breath, it was all I could do not to choke.

"I look for Moussa," I said in French, trying to breathe and look calm at the same time.

Hulk's eyes widened. "Moussa?"

"Yes. Moussa here?" My French had deteriorated to basics. I motioned to the back door of what I took to be the restaurant's kitchens. The odour of boiled rice with a thick undertone of stewed meat seeped out of the open window. I was hungry, but it didn't appeal and almost made me retch.

"Who you?"

"Me, friend Dave. Tell him, Dave."

He looked at me. He had hard eyes and an open mouth full of blackened teeth.

"Hotel Sahara. Room 221."

"GO!" he screamed. "No Moussa here."

SIXTEEN

Sue wanted to stay in the hospital with Liz, and Farid was talking to the police. I was alone in a room used for sleeping or fucking, but not for sitting and waiting. It had unappealing, brownish grease-stained wallpaper and a garish picture of a smiling camel sitting on a dune. The rear window looked onto the hotel's back-yard, where they stored all the junk: filthy mattresses, broken bed frames, overflowing bins of wood, and bulging plastic bags.

An hour passed. I decided to have a shower in the semi-clean bathroom. On entering, I switched on the light and watched, disgusted, as twenty or so cockroaches scuttled under the bathtub.

Red blotches on the tub looked like blood stains, and I imagined someone slitting their wrists and lying with their lifeblood ebbing slowly into the cooling water. I was exhausted. Liz was in the hospital, yet we had no real idea of her condition. I turned on the shower but couldn't stop looking at those red stains. An image of a man lying in the bath, his wrists slit, a half-empty bottle of whiskey, with blood puddling on the floor flashed into my mind. Then I remembered a young woman lying on the desert, all her dignity gone as the biker tried to breathe oxygen into her lungs.

Standing under the tepid water trickling over my head, I tried to re-awaken a desire to live. But it wasn't cold enough, and the grime in the bathtub made me feel dirty. It all seemed so hopeless: *Liz, my closest friend, lying in a coma. Her repressed Englishness had disappeared, replaced by bright light, laughter, and love for Moussa and life itself. Now she's dying.* The thought terrified me, as there was nothing I could do.

My thoughts turned to Moussa. *Where was he?* I waited because I knew he would come and waiting for him gave me a reason to continue breathing. I talked to Sue on the phone, but she insisted on staying with Liz at the hospital. I remained alone in the room, drinking whiskey to dull the pain and forget the images of death.

Hours passed. I dozed fitfully, then woke hungover and heavy and looked out at the town, watching as the sky darkened. Lights like flickering flames from a scattering of candles stretched into the intense drabness. *What is Moussa afraid of? Why isn't he here?* I had no answers. All I could do was wait.

Hours later, I heard a quiet knock at the door. In a stupor, I stumbled to open it. "Moussa," I said softly, looking up and down the corridor, "Come in."

We grabbed each other, crying tears of total devastation and fear—fear of the future, for Liz, for ourselves, and fear of the unknown. Hugging him, I led him to the bed and we sat down. Tears streamed down our faces. We couldn't let go. We were both devastated, but just being together helped a little.

Choking, with his voice broken and cracking with emotion, he explained, "Liz? How is she? Did you see her?"

"Yes, Sue is with her. But she's still . . ."

"I can't go to hospital. Something is wrong."

"What?"

"The police? I do not know who I can trust. I must get those men. I will have revenge."

Those last words were said with energy, passion, and anger I'd never seen Moussa display. He stood up and paced around the room. The normally quiet, fun-loving guy I knew had gone.

"Those bastards," he spat out the words. "Those fucking bastards. They shot her. We see him, remember?"

"Who? I don't remember. Who? Where?"

"Francois. Following. In the crowd. Goat Head town we called it. Remember?"

Moussa suddenly dropped to the floor, dragging me with him, and crawled across to the window. Standing up, hidden by the wall, he closed the curtains.

"Why are they open?" he cried out in desperation. "Why open? Is it signal? Are you?" His eyes widened, fear and anger piercing me with his once soft and loveable—now terrified—brown eyes.

"It's OK. I'm sorry. I didn't think. Come on, you know me, Moussa. I'm here to help you. We are brothers."

I helped him sit back on the bed again, the only place in the room to sit comfortably. It was a stark room with little furniture. It had a single high-backed chair and a small round table, cracked and blackened with cigarette burns, showing how people treated the table and the room with contempt. I tried to soothe Moussa and held his hands to comfort and calm him.

He collapsed onto the bed. "I must sleep. I am too tired. Let me sleep."

"Of course. Sleep. We can talk in the morning."

I lay down on the bed myself. Too much stress and worry had drained all my energy. My mind whirled with all the questions I hadn't asked, but as I closed my eyes I fell into a bliss of darkness to the sound of Moussa's heavy, erratic breathing.

A soft, muted light penetrating the room through the drawn curtains and slow, regular breathing woke me. The room was hot and stuffy, but I felt the person next to me was different. Glancing to my right, I saw long brown hair and a slender body curled under the sheets. "Sue?" I shook her. "Sue, wake up. Where's Moussa? What happened?"

"Coffee. Please, darling."

We had brought our bags, a camping stove, and a pot for boiling water into the room. I busied myself making coffee while

Sue struggled to wake. She staggered into the bathroom and later emerged, having showered, as she said, in lukewarm, slightly rust-coloured water.

"Moussa has gone. He left early this morning. When I got back to the room, I discovered him in your bed and woke him up. We went into Farid's room next door and talked."

"What time?" I don't know why the time mattered. I blurted it out without thinking.

"I don't know, late . . . early? He was in a state of nervous exhaustion."

"How's Liz?" I asked, suddenly remembering.

"She's in a coma and who knows if she'll wake up. I don't know what we can do. Contact the embassy?"

There was too much to take in. Thoughts of Moussa and then Liz jumped back and forth in my brain.

"When I saw him," Sue continued in a flat, tired voice, "he was quite paranoid, talking about having seen Francois. He's gone mad with anger. He left saying he had to kill Francois and Jean Jacques because they betrayed him."

"We have to stop him. How did they betray him?"

"He talked a lot last night. I can't . . ."

"Was Farid there?"

"You know, I have to tell you this. Moussa and I . . . He was so desperate . . . crying in my arms, and suddenly we were dragging each other's clothes off. Moussa needed reassurance—to know he was alive. He was despairing and longing. I . . ."

I groaned, knowing I could never match his lovemaking, but I felt so blessed Sue even looked at me. *Accept things as they are.*

"He made me promise to tell you, not because he was betraying you, but he wanted you to know he loves us all. He said sorry he hadn't had time to talk to you."

"I don't understand what is happening." I felt lost with a sense of desperation for Moussa.

"He is in a terrible state. He left, saying he would kill those French bastards. He had information from the café where you'd seen him."

"Why didn't he speak to me?"

"I guess he couldn't risk it. He's gone underground. He wants to kill Francois and Jean Jacques. Get revenge."

Drinking the coffee, black with lots of sugar, I began to recover from the trauma. There was a quiet knock on the connecting door, and Farid edged in.

"Mmm, coffee. Any left?" He helped himself as I gestured at the pot.

Farid told us the police had captured two of the gun smugglers: they were from Mali. He said they had questioned them well into the night. I didn't want to know how, but I wasn't too conflicted as they would have tried to kill us.

"They are, how do you say, little fish? They know little. We have their trucks and most of the guns they try to smuggle. Some police are involved, but we don't know who, or is that whom, teacher?"

He looked across at me. I couldn't even answer. Worrying about Liz and Moussa consumed my thoughts.

"Did you see Moussa when you got back last night?" I asked, looking directly at him, wanting to see how he reacted.

"No. Was he here? Where is he?" His voice betrayed him. I noticed him glance at Sue, almost asking permission.

"You did see him. Didn't you? Stop treating me like an idiot. Sue has already told me."

Sue responded, laughing a little. "He walked in while Moussa and I were making love. You should have seen his face."

She laughed again, and I couldn't help but to join in laughing at the absurdity of the situation and as a way of relieving the stress.

Then Farid said, "I came in, saw them, said sorry, and went into bathroom to shower. I waited until they finish." He went red, looking embarrassed, and lowered his head.

"OK. Tell me what is happening. I'm the only one who has no idea what is going on. What are we going to do? He hasn't told me anything, and what about Liz? She could be dying at this very moment."

Sue jumped up, "Liz! God, I forgot for a minute. I've got to get to the hospital. I'll take a taxi. Talk. Back around lunchtime."

Before she left, she leaned over and kissed me, whispering, "I know you love Moussa. It's OK. We all do. I love you too, sweetheart."

Her breath, those murmured words, and the image of Moussa and Sue making love made me desperate for her. *Was I second best?* I felt envious but loved him, too. Closing my eyes and breathing deeply to control my thoughts, I tried to empty my mind. Sue left without looking back.

Farid looked at me and then spoke. "Moussa is determined to kill Jean Jacques and Francois. He hates them. He said they and some Malians shot at the truck and hit Liz. All he can think about is killing them." Farid paused and looked at me to determine if I understood.

I nodded. "Go on."

"He has contacts with the police. They told him border police are waiting at frontiers and will stop them. We . . . the police will not chase them, just report as they cross checkpoints."

"What's the 'we,' Farid? Are you police as well?"

"No. I'm helping because my father . . ." Farid realized he had again said something he shouldn't have. He looked at me with a *what-have-I-said-now?* look on his face.

"What? Is your father here? Oh, fuck, man. What aren't you telling me?"

"It is best not to know. Yes, he is here. I should not have said. But he's here because it started in Bou Saâda. You must not tell anyone. Remember, he is FLN."

"Can I trust you?" Conflicted, like Moussa, I didn't know who I could have confidence in.

"Dave, I will never hurt you, Liz, or Sue. I swear. You are my best friends. My father, he wants to find Moussa. But first he must look for the Resist group trying to overthrow the government." He trailed off, desperate and almost tearful.

I looked into his eyes, and I could see a bewildered, vulnerable young man. He was eighteen now and, like me, experiencing a world getting more and more dangerous and out of control. "I'm going to go after Moussa," I said. "Find him and stop him from doing something stupid."

"I come with you," Farid said immediately.

"No. You stay here and look after Liz and Sue. Contact the British Embassy and get Liz flown out on a medical flight. Sue too. With your contacts, you can arrange things."

"No, not on your own. It is dangerous."

As I desperately threw things into my bags and tried to think about what I needed. Farid kept getting in the way, and arguing with me, and it was slowing me down.

"Look, I need you here. I don't want Sue to come—it's too dangerous."

"I have friend who can look after Sue and Liz. He will arrange all. You don't speak Arabic. I must come with you."

I picked up the coffee pot and rushed into the bathroom to wash it out. I needed time to think. I called out, "Is your friend FLN?"

"No, police. I trust him. From Bou Saâda. He can leave messages at checkpoints. I want to stop Moussa from being killed."

Farid is right. We should go together, but isn't it too dangerous for him? I walked back into the bedroom and looked directly at

Farid. "You're young, and what about your father? Will he let you go?"

He walked closer to me. He had tears in his eyes. "Moussa is my cousin. I will tell my father later. I must go. You cannot stop me."

He's right, I can't do this alone, and I can't stop him. "OK. We leave as soon as possible. See your friend. I'll pack and talk to Sue when she gets back. She won't like it, but I can't stay here and let Moussa get farther away. Why can I trust your friend from Bou Saâda?"

"Dave, you are here over a year, and this is a question you ask? These Southerners, they not our tribe. My friend is Ouled Naïl—Bou Saâdi tribe."

SEVENTEEN

We had to think about the routes Moussa and the Frenchmen would take. There were quite a few possibilities:

The main highway north to In Saleh is almost 700 kilometres. Then east to Reganne and farther north to Béni Abbès. These were roads where police patrols could stop them. Likely? Not really.

The road north out of Tam and then west on the N55A toward Abalessa could work. At Silet, the track splits south to Tinzaouaten at the frontier with Mali—dangerous and hardly travelled.

It's 165 kilometres north to Tin Massao, then it splits. The northerly route is 290 kilometres to Bordj Mokhtar, then a border crossing post with Mali. This track is forbidden and military. Highly dangerous. Unlikely. The Algerian authorities could easily stop them. It would be a suicidal drive into the wilderness on their own; they'd need gas and supplies. They may be relying on help down the road and then being smuggled out secretly, but again that was unlikely and needed a lot of coordination.

Head south on the N1, the main route out of Tam—border post at In Guezzam with Niger. They'd merge with Sahara travellers and hitch a ride on the large trucks for 400 kilometres. Then the tracks heading south spread out. The obvious route—quickest if they could avoid Algerian security. There were places to cross with no passport control. But since it was so remote and open, they could also be easily seen by spotter planes.

The final option—east to Djanet on the N55, a well-used track—took travellers to rock engravings. South to the border was under 200 kilometres, then into Niger and south to Agadez. As a route for trucks, it might be possible, and they could hide amongst the travellers.

We felt sure it would be toward Djanet. It was the safest, easiest and most accessible.

◆ ◆ ◆

Leaving Tam wasn't easy. Sue was conflicted, wanting to see Liz safely back to the UK but not wanting to lose Moussa or me. But knowing how reckless he could be, she knew we had to try to save Moussa from himself.

"I'll take care. Farid is with me. He's a careful guy, not crazy like Moussa."

"I know, but I love you. I can't lose you."

This was an emotional moment. Sue had said "I love you" many times and, looking at her, I knew it was true. My feelings were just as intense. Alone, we were lost. Sue was my rock, and together we could shield each other from the world. I didn't know what she was thinking, but I could see the desperation and longing in her eyes.

"I have to go after him. I'd never forgive myself if we leave him. He's like a brother to me."

We kissed—for the last time? It was passionate and bittersweet, and Sue's tears mingled with mine as we embraced, hoping we would meet again. I wanted—no, needed—all of us back together like before.

Farid's friend, the Bou Saâdi policeman, had been standing a little distance from us, and I hadn't really paid him much notice. But as I turned to leave, he walked forward and picked up Sue's bag. He looked familiar as he smiled and said, "Sir, go now. Your wife safe with me." *Sami*. Our hands touched as he picked up the bags, but I couldn't say anything to him. I had to go. I had to trust him.

Farid revved the Land Rover's engine. He waved to Sue, and I jumped in, shouting, "I love you."

"Be careful," she called back as I climbed into Bruce.

I watched as Sami escorted Sue to his military Jeep to take her back to the hospital.

I asked Farid again about his friend, "Do you trust him?"

"Yes, I know his father. We were friends at school. He is like a brother. Why?"

"You know he checked us in Algiers at the briefing?"

"Yes, I know. There are only a few people we trust. All Bou Saâdis."

◆ ◆ ◆

We took the main highway at first and stopped at all the checkpoints leaving Tam. The police at the checkpoint to Djanet confirmed two Frenchmen and two Malians had passed their post and then, about four hours later, Moussa had sped by.

Now we knew they had decided to head east to Djanet, and they wouldn't be too obvious by heading south across the border into Niger. What they didn't reckon on was the efficiency of the Algerian police. For the moment, Farid told us the police wanted to maintain a low profile and merely observe what they were doing.

The tarmac stopped, and we hit the *piste*, which was like corrugated iron. Bruce shook us and the contents up, no matter how fast I pushed him. We sped past oasis settlements, mud houses, and palm trees shimmering in the distance.

EIGHTEEN

It took one-and-a-half days of driving. Sometimes the track disappeared, and we had to cast around looking for other routes heading in the right direction. It was impossible to appreciate what has been described as the magnificent scenery of endless, barren dunes and craggy mountains. They registered as a blur, and even now I can't remember much about them. Finally, we arrived in Djanet at around three in the afternoon and turned into the main square: a few sunbaked buildings, a man dozing in the shade, and a goat chewing on a piece of cardboard. An older-style French colonial hotel, *Hôtel de l'Oasis Rouge* was on one side of the open, dusty square. It was well past lunchtime, and as the hotel restaurant was closed, we ate at a non-descript, hole-in-the-wall café next door: chops, a stew of beans, and stale bread. Flies crawled over the table, landed on the food, and flew in our faces until we relinquished our plates to them.

In the evening, we watched the pre-packaged tourists arriving at their authentic lodgings—round, mud-plastered huts with palm-leaf roofs. At five the next day, they sped off in their appointed Land Rovers and Land Cruisers on guided tours of the petroglyphs. The rock engravings were world-famous, and I would have loved to see them. But this was a different mission: we had to find Moussa. Farid spent the rest of the day trying to get some information from the police about Moussa or the French, but there was no news.

The second morning, getting more frustrated, we sat at a café table having a breakfast of bread, dates, and coffee opposite the police and customs post. Across from us, a bright red and yellow Mercedes diesel truck piled high with sacks of dates was loading its passengers. Some thirty men in long, deep purple Tuareg robes were desperately scrambling up the sides to claim a place on top. It was one of the trucks taking the route to Mali, Niger, and on to Agadez.

We watched them shouting and tossing their bags up to their friends already installed on top of the truck. Everyone wore a white or purple *shesh*: a head covering of cotton worn like a turban, wrapped around their heads as a protection against the heat, dust, and blistering sun. It left only the eyes visible but made them look mysterious.

As they approached the vehicle, each man presented his passport. The policeman gave a cursory look, then motioned to the truck. Even though Farid told me the police had a picture of Jean Jacques and Francois, they didn't seem too concerned about checking everyone's passports. It would have been easy for them to clamber onto one of these trucks in disguise and disappear.

However, they must have disposed of their vehicle. We had searched all the garages in this dust-strewn town. Farid had checked with the police, but we couldn't find any trace of it. Of course, many smashed-up trucks and cars had been abandoned, and their vehicle could have been sold for scrap and quickly broken up or hidden in one of the shuttered workshops. There had been no sighting of Moussa, apart from the one on the road three days ago as he headed toward Djanet.

Farid told me the police weren't interested in looking for him, as their priority was hunting down the terrorists. He mentioned they had heard reports of a gunfight farther east yesterday evening. That very morning we'd watched four open-topped Jeeps with heavy machine guns speed off in the direction the fighters were said to have gone.

Farid spoke with despair in his eyes. "They told me something more."

"What?" I asked, fearful because deep down I knew. "Liz?" my voice cracked with dread for the news I couldn't—no, didn't—want to hear. He nodded.

"She's . . . She's . . . gone?"

"Yes, last night in hospital." Farid reached over and took my hand. "I'm so sorry, Dave. We all loved her. She was so . . ."

"Sue?"

"She said, bring Moussa back."

We sat for a while without speaking, lost in our own thoughts of anguish and grief. *Everything is falling apart. Alone in Djanet. Deserted by Touati. We've lost control. Liz is dead.*

Remembering Liz on the hospital bed made me shudder and cry tears of hopelessness. Numb and lost, I felt utter panic.

"We need to pay for information," Farid said, looking at me, knowing I was desperate. "Someone must know. Now I go to the *souk* and ask the traders. I tell them we are giving reward for information about Moussa. We have to find him."

I was exhausted, drained of energy, and lacked the will or energy to go on. The police weren't bothered, and Farid's connections didn't extend all this way down south. He must have known my spirit was dying, as he had to push and cajole me, then half carry me back to the hotel, where I fell onto the bed and blacked out.

Some hours later, Farid returned, shook me awake and handed me a can of Coca-Cola. It was cold and had the sugar to revive me. He had also bought me a *shesh*. Getting me to stand in front of the mirror, he wound yards of lilac cotton around my head. I disappeared into the reflected eyes of a Tuareg. It hid my face so I could retreat and guard my thoughts. It gave me confidence, as I could hide my misery and fear and be less conscious of staring eyes.

He dressed me: long white cotton underpants and a purple cotton robe the men wore. Farid called it a *gandoura*. Instead of a Westerner, when I looked in the mirror, I became a Tuareg warrior. With a final flourish, he gave me a pair of mirrored sunglasses.

Then he told me the news. A villager had talked about a man who had been wounded in a shootout in the desert. He had been taken to a small oasis settlement about 200 kilometres from Djanet. Farid had vague directions, but the informant was willing to come with us so he could return to his village. Farid said we would only pay him if this man existed. He told him that the villagers didn't want to inform the police, as they were afraid they would be blamed for wounding him. They didn't know what to do, and Farid had to swear to keep it secret.

An hour later, we met our guide standing by the Land Rover outside the hotel. Farid called him Goma but told me it wasn't his real name, as he was terrified the village would be held responsible for the shooting. Goma wore the Tuareg's long purple gandoura, with a black *shesh* wound around his head, looking the same as the men who ambled around town.

NINETEEN

The journey down was fraught. The informant, Goma, insisted on driving. As he knew where the police checkpoints were, he could avoid them.

This added time to the trip and only increased my anxiety. I wanted to drive as fast as possible to get to the village. *Is Goma kidnapping us to sell us for a fortune he can hardly imagine? Is all this an elaborate scam to get a free ride back home? If there is no one there, what will we do?* My mind was racing, and even conferring with Farid didn't help. He was as clueless as me but kept on saying it was worth the risk. He trusted this man driving up steep slopes and then along dune crests and down the slopes like a professional.

I was distracted by the beauty of the desert; it was still hot, but in the late afternoon light the orange-red sands seemed pure— untouched by man. The dunes stretched out before us like an undulating sea. There was no indication anyone had passed this way, apart from a few tire tracks. Goma showed great skill nego- tiating a route through this barren but awe-inspiring arid land. I couldn't see any features he could use as a directional beacon. Yet he drove confidently, following a series of snake like-trails running in a southerly direction.

But after hours of driving on the corrugated surface, our bodies shaken to almost unbearable limits, I wanted to scream, preoccupied with another kind of agony.

Eventually, we turned off the main *piste* to follow the spoor of a few other cars travelling east, skirting the mountains and driving along a wide river valley.

The heat in the air sapped the moisture and energy from our bodies. I had a splitting headache, and one part of me wanted to lie down and forget the pain and anguish. We drove on, and I said nothing. I had no control over the situation. *Inshallah*, it is God's will, and who knows what will happen? It has already been written. One aspect of my Western-educated brain couldn't accept that, but the rest of me gave up and I decided: *You've got to do this for Moussa.* I surrendered to the inevitable and let events take over.

On nearing Goma's village, we entered an oasis settlement surrounded by palm trees and vegetable gardens. The houses were all built of the local mud and blended into the landscape. After journeying for about five hours in the sand and rock-strewn desert, it was magical—a village lost in time. I asked the name, and Farid shrugged, but at least the pain of sitting and being shaken to the very core had stopped.

Goma drove up to a makeshift hut and talked to the older men in Tamahaq, the Tuareg dialect spoken in southern Algeria and stretching across borders not recognized by the Tuareg desert nomads. Farid didn't understand a word, so we were both dependent on our guide. One man replied and motioned to the hut where they served hot, sweet mint tea. My hosts refilled my glass until satiated; I politely shook the empty glass three times before putting it down with a murmured Arabic *shukran*. (Thank you.)

The tea and a couple of painkillers revived me. I was slowly recovering and desperate to see this wounded man, but Farid told me to be patient. It was custom to establish good relations, but also for them to see if they could trust us. Frustration was hardly the word for my distress, but I put on a smile, nodded, and shook my head—playing at being polite.

The sun was setting. The evening light, called *asir*, was soft and enchanting. It gave a golden glow to the mud houses and the deep pink desert sand. It was cooler now, and after our hosts had prayed, we left the hut to be shown the village and hopefully taken to Moussa. In the soft receding light, everything was more precise and sharper. After escaping the desert's bleakness, I could appreciate the peace and calm settling after a long, hot day. Birds twittered and called, and I looked up at a tangle of pigeons whirling and twisting over the trees.

It was all in stark contrast to the silent emptiness of the arid desert we had just left. The air was softer. Breathing in, I sensed the water trickling past in the narrow, twisting canals and the aroma of damp fertile soil. Here in this paradise of an oasis, I relaxed and willed myself to adopt the *inshallah* complex, "what will be, will be—it is God's will."

We walked down narrow, winding streets—the buildings on either side providing much-needed shade. Now, as the long, hot day folded into the evening, men lounged on their doorsteps, exchanging gossip with their neighbours, resting in the evening after a hard day's work.

Here, they trade with Mali and Niger and have little in common with the lighter-skinned Arabs farther north. The Tuaregs in this village dressed in their traditional clothing of long flowing gowns and head coverings with only the whites of their eyes showing. It is easy to understand why, after travelling in the desert and breathing in the fine dust particles.

We *salaamed* them as we passed, and they returned our greetings, inviting us for tea, but we refused politely. Some of the men gently chastised the giggling little melee of boys and girls following us. My identity as a European had been outed, but Farid said they were not offended; rather they admired my effort to become like them, if only in clothing.

Some houses had been dug out of the rock, with a door to indicate a dwelling. Inside, Farid told me, they had a few niches cut into the interior rock walls for storage jars. Water is the village's lifeblood, and a watercourse of small canals ran along the paths, just above street level. The men open the narrow channels to allow the water to flood their vegetable gardens. Farid told me the water came from the distant mountains and flowed through deep underground channels dug thousands of years ago. He called it a *falaj* system and explained it was strictly regulated. Each area of land got a regulated amount of water.

On this grand tour, we followed our guide walking down a gentle slope to the palmeraies. I was fascinated by the village and looked at the men sitting on their doorsteps. Whenever I waved a hand in greeting, they waved back, calling out to us in Tamahaq. But this tour was becoming frustrating, as I felt we were walking in circles.

"Come on, Farid, we've got to find out if this is Moussa."

"Be patient, I am also anxious, but we show our respect for the village. They are watching us."

I greeted a young man bent over shovelling sand away from the door of his house. *"As Salam Alaikum."*

"Wa Alaikum Salam." He returned the "peace be upon you" Arabic greeting and waved. Then he bent to shovel again.

"Good," said Farid. "We can't rush them. Life is in different speed here."

My desperation to see Moussa ate away at me. Time crept on, obscuring the past, just like the desert silently entombing the gardens.

Each garden had its quota of date palm trees, with patches of vegetables growing in the tree's shade: carrots, onions, and green-leaved mint. I picked a leaf and rubbed it between my fingers. The comforting aroma assailed my long-starved senses. A few desultory-looking goats munched on scraps of paper and chickens scratched and clucked, then—running bandy-legged at our approach—scolded us for disturbing them.

The need to see Moussa was overwhelming. *When will this charade stop? I know not to show my impatience, but I can't do this . . .*

"Farid, please."

"I think we are closer now."

We passed the women washing at the communal washhouse, slapping and pounding the mounds of clothing onto the rocks worn smooth by hundreds of years of slapping and scrubbing. They saw us and, giggling among the suds, dropped the clothes and turned to wave and watch. We waved, greeted them, and walked on. The soapy water flowed down the channels to the palms.

Breathing and corralling my negativity, I challenged myself to *live in the moment.* I looked across the pristine dunes drifting down to a ksar of ruined turrets and broken walls of mud and stone, a sandy, flat, palm-tree studded plain, and in the far distance, cliffs. Transfixed by the atmosphere of the soft evening light, I noticed the fine dust sparkling as it was transformed into dancing golden flecks by the dying rays of the sun.

I was calm and at peace when we eventually arrived in a small sandy square with houses made of palm branches, caked with mud, and thatched with palm leaves. Here, in a gloomy room, rows of black pots gleamed like polished coal where the fading light from the one window struck them. It was sunbaked red mud glazed black, but the vases were sensuous, smooth, and silky to touch. The pottery supplied the tourist trade, and I felt obliged to buy two long-necked jugs. Now, having endured the tour and showing we were not there to disparage them or be discourteous, our guides led us to the wounded man in a backroom: A body slumped on a wooden bed. We shuffled inside this gloomy room, with streaks of fading light slanting through gaps in the branches forming the walls.

"Moussa? Moussa, are you OK? It's Farid and me."

He grunted when I said his name. What had become of him?

Farid spoke in Arabic and translated. Moussa had lost his ability to communicate and mostly croaked an answer. He asked for water, which we gave him, and he smoked some foul-smelling, hand-rolled cigarette. Farid told me the villagers said it was to relieve the pain. There was a smell of decay emanating from him. Flies buzzed excitedly around his legs. Unshaven, Moussa was a mess. We wanted to take him away, but he kept refusing as if he were in some euphoric state.

Farid talked with the people in the hut and told me they had heard the rapid-fire of machine guns from a mountain to the south. One of the villagers had a truck and, after the gunfire had finished, they drove off to see what had happened.

They had found Moussa crawling on the ground, crippled and covered in blood. The settlement didn't have a doctor or communication with the outside world. They feared taking him into town, so to be careful they had sent Goma to Djanet to find help. Farid told me they were afraid of being arrested for something they hadn't done—a wounded man and no explanation. They knew all too well the vagaries of the police in Djanet.

We wanted to leave the village soon, and Farid persuaded them to let us take Moussa to a hospital. He told me to get the Land Rover, and Goma came with me and guided me back across a dried-up riverbed and into the square in front of the house.

The crescent moon provided a ghostly light as the men lifted Moussa's inert body into the back of the Land Rover and laid him carefully on a mattress, with a pillow for his head. One of the men placed a blanket over him and a goatskin water carrier beside him.

It was now dark, but we wanted to leave the village as soon as we could. The moon gave us some light, and Goma clambered in to guide us back to the main piste. There he left us with many "salaams" and exhortations of *"Adhhab bisalam."* ("Go in peace.")

TWENTY

After a couple of nightmarish hours driving on washboard ridges, we decided to stop and make camp as Moussa kept on screaming.

Without radio contact, we couldn't call for help. Farid made a small fire, and while I cradled Moussa in my arms near the flickering flames, he rolled up Moussa's cotton *djebella* so we could see and treat his wounds. His legs were swollen, but they had been cleaned and bandaged with pieces of fabric and herbal leaves. Even so, the putrid smell of rotting flesh made me gag. Brownish pus oozed from his wounds. His skin was cold and shiny, with black and blue patches: gangrene.

Moussa was delirious and calling for Liz. We had some whiskey, and I asked Farid to get it. He returned with the bottle and some water as well. Moussa swallowed a few drops of water but started coughing and choking. I used the whiskey to clean his wounds, hoping to kill the bacteria with the alcohol. Then we washed and dressed them as well as we could with our limited medical supplies.

Our dilemma was either driving on in the dark, with Moussa screaming in agony and saying we were trying to kill him, or to stop, then continue in the morning at a slower pace.

I held his warm body in my arms and wept. The gaping wounds had reopened, and blood soaked through the makeshift bandages and dripped into the sand. We couldn't do much, not here in the emptiness and silence of the Sahara. A crescent moon floated above us, and our fire sputtered and crackled.

We'd become intense friends and lovers, sharing a passionate enjoyment of life, but now his body lay helpless in my arms. I sobbed as I watched his life spirit ebb away.

"I want sleep," he implored.

"Moussa, I'm here. So is Farid. Liz is OK. She's in hospital. We're taking you there to be next to her. Liz is fine. You know how much she loves you. In the morning we'll find the road and get you to the hospital. I love you, man. Talk to me. What happened?"

He spoke in Arabic, and Farid translated, "He says he wants Liz. You heard him saying her name over and over. He found them camping in an oued."

I nodded, holding Moussa's head, wiping it with a wet cloth. He shivered violently, then—overcome—shook and convulsed with a coughing fit. I held him and put a damp cloth on his head. My tears fell on his upturned face, and he must have felt them because he laughed and then gulped air. I looked at Farid, who had a look of despair. We both knew Moussa was dying but couldn't say anything.

Farid continued, "He had been following car tracks and knew it was them. I don't know how he knew. Francois, Jean Jacques, and two others—Malians probably."

"What else did he say?" I asked desperately.

Moussa turned his head and looked at me. "Hello. Dave."

"Moussa."

"You trying kill me. Driving." He started to laugh, but this turned to a racking cough.

"Here, drink." I poured droplets of water into his mouth, but most of it dribbled down his chin. His wheezing chilled me.

Farid took the bottle of water away and held Moussa's hand. "We shouldn't make him talk. It's not good for him. We need bigger fire. I will get more wood. Don't make him talk. Please."

Farid was a gentle soul. I knew we shouldn't push Moussa into talking, but I needed to know what had happened.

Moussa looked at me again. "I shot Francois. *Salo*." He spat the word out, hoarse and gulping air. "He killed Liz. I know it. I love her."

"I know. Stay quiet. Don't talk." Moussa was delirious. It was so painful to see the man I adored reduced to such a state.

"I want . . . How," another burst of coughing. "How—Liz?"

"She's fine." I lied. "In the hospital in Tam. We'll take you there."

He looked at me. His deep brown eyes pierced into me. "I not see her," he said. "Not this life. I want to die."

"Please, we need you. Liz, me, Farid, Sue. We all need you making us laugh, making us love you."

"I not kill Jean Jacques." He stopped breathing rapidly. "You kill him." He looked intently at me, and I nodded. "Yes, I will." Satisfied, Moussa turned his head away, "I sleep now."

I put my coat under his head and positioned him carefully. Farid piled the wood to make a blaze close to Moussa, then heated a can of soup over the flames. We ate, but as Moussa was sleeping, we didn't disturb him. A cloud slipped in front of the waning moon—the only light from the flickering flames—drawing me into an agonizing alternative reality.

I had a restless, cold night, but I must have fallen into a deep sleep because in the ghostly, grey pre-dawn when I woke, Moussa had gone. I shouted at Farid to wake up, and following his tracks, we clambered up the dune face crying out: "Moussa. Moussa."

He was on the other side, having rolled down the slope, and was lying on his back staring up at the sky. His body felt cold, with no pulse. Weeping, we fell to the ground.

Later, looking up at the awakening day, my mind drifted to a wedding celebration we'd seen.

We could hear the rhythmic beating of skin-taut drums calling us—we ran—then entranced, watched—standing so close we could see the sweat beading on the drummers' faces—smell the energy and vigor—others danced and shouted in the night, spinning their guns—then firing their ancient rifles—a terrific bang shook the air—so loud it made you jump—an acrid smell of gunpowder and white trails of smoke floating upwards—in the dark, the flickering flames of hand-held torches reflected and shimmered on the shiny, bare arms of the dancers held high—they were jet-black—their skin contrasted with their white flowing robes—a purple shesh wound around their heads, covering all but the gleaming whites of their eyes—they swayed and leaped as they moved wildly round and round—stamping their feet in time with the rhythmic beating of the drums—the heartbeat of pristine Africa—earthy, wild, remote—Moussa dancing—hands and arms waving and circling—loving every second—smiling, laughing—everyone clapping with the beat and passion of the dance—Moussa twirling and laughing.

AFTERWORD

In Vancouver, Farid talked about our friendship and some of the things we had experienced. Then on his last night, as we sat on the hotel balcony overlooking the harbour's calm waters and the mountains, he plucked up the courage to make his big reveal. As he was leaving the next day, he must have felt this was his last chance.

"I'm not sure how to say this, but about five years ago, I cleared out my father's papers after he died. I found a file the FLN had written on you. He had kept it in his safe and must have forgotten about it." Farid paused and closed his eyes for a few seconds.

"I'm sorry, Farid. How old was he?"

"Almost seventy."

I waited for him to continue. "Can I get you anything? A glass of water?"

"No, thank you." He took a deep breath.

"A file on me?" *Of course, they had one. I would really like to read it.* "Anything else? One on Sue? Moussa? How much did they know about me and Moussa or me and Sue or . . .?"

"Wait. I found the file, and over these last five years I worked hard connecting the dots. I can call you a lynchpin. I think this is the right word. Without you . . ."

"What?" I pressed, shocked at his use of the word. "I thought I was just a tiny cog in a vast machine."

"Remember, Seamus was deported. He went off with JJ, some other French teachers, and two young Algerian men to a drinking session. He got drunk and talked about how the French trusted him, and he could make a lot of money selling information. One of the Algerians reported him to the police. They didn't like him being so superior."

"Yeah, I know." I laughed. "He was . . . what did Liz call him? 'An utter bore.'"

"Right." Farid continued. "So, when arrested, they found he had papers from the French Embassy. The OAS, The Organisation Armée Secrète. The OAS? Oh, you may not know, they are far-right group that fought against French government giving Algeria Independence. They wanted to pay back the FLN by making a coup to destroy the government."

"OAS? Yes, I read about them. A really powerful group in France close to people in the government. Then of course, De Gaulle and his betrayal of the *Pieds-Noir*."

"Right. The *Sûreté* discovered this plot to overthrow our government, but didn't know much more. When they took Seamus, JJ was also arrested, but they persuaded him to work with us. He knew Francois, and there was ill-feeling between the two. Something going back to Paris and Beau."

I picked up the bottle of wine. This was going to be a long night. "Shall we go inside? The wind picks up and it gets cold."

We moved into the suite attached to the bedroom. I sat on the sofa, facing Farid to observe how he reacted when I asked him questions.

"Should I continue? Yes?"

"Please do." His question sounded a little officious. But I liked Farid, and I wanted to know more.

"They couldn't have JJ contact the Embassy directly. It was too dangerous. You were British and neutral, and friendly with Moussa."

Farid looked at me, and I detected a flitting glimpse of guilt flashing across his face.

"They knew a lot about you. Sue, your American girlfriend. Oh, and you taught at the same school as JJ. This made it easier for him to have reason to contact you."

"Anything else in the file?" Farid shook his head. "It's OK. You were only eighteen and doing what your dad asked you to. I trusted you. We were friends, all of us."

Farid shifted in his chair. I wanted to reassure him that I didn't blame him or hold him responsible.

"Do you want another drink?" I picked up the bottle of wine and shook it. "Nothing left. Give me a minute."

Farid nodded eagerly, perhaps feeling he had revealed the worst part.

I returned with a second bottle and filled both our glasses.

I needed to soften Farid up a little. He still sounded a little too formal and uptight, and I knew he had more to say about what the FLN knew about me. "JJ? I never liked him you know. I didn't trust him. He was so . . . so . . . I don't know, French and superior and too clever."

"Yes, I know."

"So," I said, "to summarize. The *Sûreté* needed someone to pass information from the Embassy to JJ and on to Francois/Henri and get information back from Resist."

"Yes. You were the obvious person, as JJ couldn't be seen with Algerians—this might destroy his cover. The reports said you were easy to persuade . . ." Again, Farid paused and looked uncomfortable.

"Oh, go on. You've started now. I'm not blaming you. Come on. Tell me. I was easy to persuade because . . .?"

"Because of your love for money and your desire for Moussa. They knew about it." He coughed, embarrassed, and looked down at the floor. "I knew you were having an affair with him. It was obvious. I didn't mind. Moussa was my cousin and I loved him. He was so much larger than life and . . ."

But their knowledge of my relationship with Moussa was embarrassing, as those kinds of affairs were unacceptable in Algeria. I suppose they needed something to threaten me with if required—the old carrot or stick approach. For a second, I thought about Sami. *Was he sent to seduce me too? Did they film us in the bedroom? No. Too much had happened after. Did Farid know about ...?*

"I remember that policeman friend of yours—he looked after Sue when we were looking for Moussa. What was his name?"

"Sami. Yes, of course. He was a friend, but I haven't seen him for years. What about him?"

"Oh, I just wanted to know how involved he was. Was he in the file?"

"No. He was police."

I asked as casually as I could, "What happened to him?"

"He's in France, I think."

I shrugged as if I wasn't too interested. I thought of Sami in his uniform but felt glad we'd kept something secret. Life had been on the edge over there. We'd been playing big men's games and had no idea what we were getting into.

"I can't forget Moussa, you know." I looked at Farid. Close to losing it, I forced myself to continue. "I think about him all the time. Even now."

Tears formed in Farid's eyes. It's incredible, forty years on, and he still had this effect on us. After a few quiet moments of silent remembrance, I asked, "Do you think they'd have used Sue too?"

"That would have been last thing if they needed to persuade you. I'm not in secret police, you know. I am just translator."

"Yes. Just get on with it." *He wheedled too much. Making excuses. How much had he changed? I knew he was FLN and with contacts to influential people in the Government, and that's how he'd got that job in New York with the UN. Our last few days had been fun; I'd thought of him as a long-lost friend, but why is he telling me all this now?*

"It has taken years to find all this out. It was difficult. Some papers from Touati's files. The plotters could have been successful. Touati emigrated to the States, did you know?"

"No, I didn't. He was good, in a way. I mean, the mission was successful, wasn't it?"

"Yes. It was. The papers you handed over detailed contacts in the French Embassy and high-level French Government officials authorized them. But they were never prosecuted. It was—how do you say—hushed up?"

"Yes. So, the *Sûreté* passed false info to me and on through JJ to Henri in Resist, and then he passed stuff back through me. What else? What about Liz getting shot?"

"It gets complicated. From what I can guess, Francois had become suspicious of you and Moussa. He was double agent—working for us and Resist. Maybe he had to give them something to prove himself. I don't know. But he was following you. Remember you thought you saw someone down south? The car crash?"

I remembered the bodies on the ground. The girl breathing her last few breaths. It was a haunting memory. As I didn't speak, Farid continued, "Francois was stupid. The older man worked with Resist. Francois used him as someone who obviously didn't look like a spy."

This was overwhelming. "Were they assassins? The woman too? She was what . . . a cover? Oh, God."

I hobbled over to the window. My legs had grown numb from sitting too long. It had turned dark outside. The lights of North Vancouver's houses and factories sparkled all the way up the sides of the mountain. It was claustrophobic in the hotel room with the doors to the balcony closed, but also comforting; the walls protected us from whatever demons lurked out there.

Farid got up and closed the curtains. Moving around helped burn off the negative energy this created, but I needed closure. Hard as it was, I wanted—no, had to see it through. I couldn't take another drink. My head was reeling. Trying to turn, I stumbled against a chair, hitting my leg. Farid moved to help me, and I hobbled my way to the bathroom.

"I'm OK, Farid. I just need to piss. I'll throw some cold water over my head. Hey, use the kettle to make us coffee. I need it."

After two coffees, I asked Farid to continue. It was way past midnight on his last night, but we both needed to complete the story.

"Francois and JJ followed us. They had contacts with the police. Remember Moussa didn't trust them. I wasn't sure so I asked my friend, Sami, a Bou Saâdi man, to help."

I sat up. Sami. His name again. I had to control my reactions and not give anything away. I spoke calmly so as not to reveal my own emotional state. "Yes. Moussa didn't trust a lot of people. He said JJ had betrayed him. So, they wanted to kill him and me because, what? We knew too much? I promised Moussa I would kill Jean Jacques, you know?"

Farid didn't respond. Maybe there are things he doesn't need to know. "Yes, he knew where we were going. One of the police insiders told them. The Malians confessed to the FLN when we caught them. JJ and Francois rushed ahead of us and intended to wait when we got to rock art site, but Moussa stumbled onto their camp and they shot at him. It was all rushed, and what? A balls-up?"

I nodded. "JJ double-crossed us, and they shot Liz by mistake?"

He nodded. "I'm sorry. We were such close friends."

"Yes, I know. You were a pillar. I was falling apart in Djanet, and you helped me get it together again. We never would have found Moussa if not for you. He knew we were there for him in his last few hours, and he died going to see Liz in the stars." I paused for a few minutes. Then I asked the question that had been bothering me. "Farid, why are you telling me all this now?"

"I want you to write about it. I can't, but . . ."

"No. I don't think so."

"Please. For Moussa, Liz, and Sue."

"Let me think about it. It's not easy, to drag up all those old memories."

◆◆◆

Farid had reopened a desire to re-evaluate what had happened. To examine what Sue, Liz, and Moussa had meant and to lay to rest their memories. It would allow me to delve into corners of my psyche that had remained buried since leaving Algeria. However, as Farid had been in New York, he didn't know the whole story. Remembering Sue and Sami, I smiled, keeping our sacred promise.

Sue had re-acquainted me with different sensations. In Britain, I'd become locked into a particular way of life. It was intoxicating in Algeria to explore a new world and reinvent myself. Moussa was gentle and compassionate in a way Steve had never been, and he listened to me as we shared our thoughts and fears. Yes, he was mercurial and could change to reflect the environment he found himself in—like a chameleon. However, he was still a soft, vulnerable person underneath.

Sue was confident and authoritative, but she told me she hadn't loved her previous husband. Ours was a genuine, open relationship. After she found out about Moussa, Sue admitted that at first, she felt jealous, but talking with Liz and arranging a threesome helped. Losing Liz, though, was one of the worst things that could have happened. Then Moussa. We were shattered, and the only comfort we had was with each other, so we stayed together with a deep understanding of love and shared experiences.

CPSIA information can be obtained
at www.ICGtesting.com
Printed in the USA
LVHW042116260422
717237LV00007B/718